A Summer in São Paulo

*These medics are leaving their hearts
in South America!*

Invited to spend the summer in the high-tech,
high-stakes world of São Paulo's premiere teaching
hospital, Hospital Universitário Paulista, it's the
chance for these visiting medical professionals to
shake off their everyday routine—and embrace the
vivacity of South America!

While they're certainly turning up the heat during
the long working days, the warm days and sultry
nights are the perfect setting for romance…
And none of them can resist the call of passion
in paradise!

Discover more in

Awakened by Her Brooding Brazilian
by Ann McIntosh

Falling for the Single Dad Surgeon
by Charlotte Hawkes

Available now!

One Hot Night with Dr. Cardoza
by Tina Beckett

Coming next month!

Dear Reader,

I absolutely loved my heroine, Flávia. She is so focused and strong willed, yet also so vulnerable, I knew she needed a very special hero to match her. And who better than a man like Jake, a man who is already turning his life upside down to take care of his late sister's son?

I had this rough plan for them…but they just ignored me. And what I really loved, as I wrote this story, was that it turned out Jake needs Flávia just as much as she needs him. Maybe more.

I hope you love Flávia—and Jake and Brady—as much I do. It's lovely hearing from readers, and you can find me on Facebook, Twitter or swing by my site at charlotte-hawkes.com.

Charlotte x

FALLING FOR THE SINGLE DAD SURGEON

CHARLOTTE HAWKES

HARLEQUIN

MEDICAL
ROMANCE

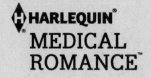

HARLEQUIN®
MEDICAL ROMANCE™

Recycling programs for this product may not exist in your area.

ISBN-13: 978-1-335-14940-4

Falling for the Single Dad Surgeon

This edition published by arrangement with Harlequin Books S.A.

For questions and comments about the quality of this book, please contact us at CustomerService@Harlequin.com.

Harlequin Enterprises ULC
22 Adelaide St. West, 40th Floor
Toronto, Ontario M5H 4E3, Canada
www.Harlequin.com

Printed in U.S.A.

Born and raised on the Wirral Peninsula in England, **Charlotte Hawkes** is mom to two intrepid boys who love her to play building block games with them, and who object loudly to the amount of time she spends on the computer. When she isn't writing—or building with blocks—she is company director for a small Anglo/French construction firm. Charlotte loves to hear from readers, and you can contact her at her website: charlotte-hawkes.com.

Books by Charlotte Hawkes

Harlequin Medical Romance

Hot Army Docs

Encounter with a Commanding Officer
Tempted by Dr. Off-Limits

The Army Doc's Secret Wife
The Surgeon's Baby Surprise
A Bride to Redeem Him
The Surgeon's One-Night Baby
Christmas with Her Bodyguard
A Surgeon for the Single Mom
The Army Doc's Baby Secret
Unwrapping the Neurosurgeon's Heart
Surprise Baby for the Billionaire

Visit the Author Profile page at Harlequin.com.

To Zena

You keep calling even when I've got lost inside my own head (or book) and forgotten to call back for the umpteenth time—I have no idea how I got lucky enough to have you!

Thank You For Being A Friend... xx

Praise for
Charlotte Hawkes

"What an interesting, fast-paced, surprising and entertaining read Ms. Hawkes takes readers on with this book where...the dialogue was riveting and...the chemistry between this couple was strong and tangible from the moment they meet."
—*Harlequin Junkie* on
Christmas with Her Bodyguard

CHAPTER ONE

THIS WOMAN WAS surely going to be his undoing.

The premonition walloped into Jake Cooper as he stared across the throng of well-heeled guests attending the welcome gala dinner for the summer programme at Brazil's renowned Hospital Universitário Paulista.

He knew it, and still he stared. And despite the colleagues jostling to talk to him, he found he couldn't draw his gaze from one agitated figure.

Flávia Maura. Or, as she was more colloquially known, the *selvagem* woman.

Wild. Savage. The jungle woman.

And there was no doubt in Jake's mind that she posed a setback to his own sanity.

She was standing in a trio of women; yet, for him, the other two had blurred into muted shades of grey around Flávia. Just as everyone else in the vast, elegant room had done, the moment he'd laid eyes on this one woman. He might have thought that there was something abruptly wrong with his vision, but for the fact that he was so focused on the image of her, in glorious high definition.

He was supposed to be here for the training

programme. A summer of top medical experts from around the world all meeting in one place both to learn, and also to teach, new cutting-edge skills to each other. Not least demonstrating the clinical trial he himself was part of, where he was using a scorpion-venom-based toxin to highlight cancer cells—effectively showing up as a fluorescent tumour paint when put under near-infrared light, within a patient on the operating table.

And Flávia Maura had been one of the researchers who had worked on the toxin he was using for his particular trial.

Only, it wasn't her professional skills which currently had his eyes devouring every inch of her, from the top of her rich, glossy hair right down to the sexy high heels in which she appeared to be trying to balance, and everything in between. Not least the long, figure-hugging metallic gown in some deep green, which seemed to shimmer to black as she moved. Everything about it teased him. The way it clung so lovingly to her body, but the shimmers tricked the eye; the way the neckline offered a mouthwatering taste—but no more—of sexy cleavage; the way the side slit, which tantalised glimpses of endlessly long legs, but never once veered into dangerous territory.

Like the merest whisper of a promise of something more.

It was ridiculous that he—who had known plenty of beautiful women during his assuredly bachelor life—should be so easily ensnared. Yet here he was, like a fish dangling helplessly from a fisherman's hook.

She looked sophisticated yet sexy. Elegant yet slightly devilish. And utterly, and completely, terrified. It wasn't just the way her eyes were darting about the room however hard she kept trying to look her colleagues in the eye. It wasn't simply how her hands kept toying with her dress, her earrings, her shoes, as if she felt completely out of her comfort zone. It wasn't even her confident smile, which froze in place just once or twice.

It was the way she kept subconsciously edging behind the shoulder of one of the other two women, as though they could somehow provide a barrier between her and the colleagues who were clearly edging to talk to her—the woman whose work as a naturalist and researcher were helping to change the face of contemporary cancer treatment.

It should have acted as a warning that he could read her—a relative stranger—so well.

It should have worried him even more that it didn't.

But then, it wasn't the first warning he'd had, was it? He'd known it three days ago, in the middle of an operation, with the guy who'd been the closest thing to a best mate for the better part of a decade.

The memory played out in his head, as if reliving that conversation could somehow help to steel him against the pull of the woman standing no more than thirty metres from him right now.

As if it could help him resist this odd lure of striding across the room and claiming her for his own all night.

Like some kind of Neanderthal that he'd never been before. Like the guy he'd sworn only three days ago that he wasn't.

'So,' his mate and neurosurgeon colleague had demanded good-naturedly partway through their joint operation. 'Who did you sleep with in order to get on to this year's summer teaching programme at Paulista's?'

'Funny, Oz.' He'd grinned but he hadn't even bothered looking up from the surgery.

His eyes had been trained on the brain of his patient as his colleague, neurosurgeon Oscar Wright, had worked to reveal a tumour. They'd made the first incision and had been drilling the bone flap as close to the tumour site as possible.

Once they were ready to start the resection, they would wake the patient and begin brain mapping. Normally, Jake wasn't in on these operations, his area of expertise being vascular oncology, but the tumour paint was *his* clinical trial. Added to that was the fact that the particular young lad in question had always been particularly jumpy and Jake had been working with him long enough to have built up a rapport that would help during the awake part of the surgery.

But in that moment, the lad was still anaesthetised and the banter he and Oz shared often made critical operations like those seem easier.

'Besides, that's more your style than mine, isn't it?'

'You think I didn't try?' Oz had shaken his head. 'I pulled out all the stops last year when they were choosing surgeons to go to Brazil, lot of good that did me. Not that it was a hardship, you understand.'

'I bet it wasn't,' Jake had retorted dryly. 'Though I imagine that high-profile case you have coming might have something to do with it.'

They had both known Oz's name would have been right up there with his if it hadn't been for the fact that Oz needed to stay in London this winter, which was summer below the equator in Brazil.

The guy's reputation as a playboy preceded him, but he was also one of the best neurosurgeons Jake had known. *Work hard, play harder*— that was Oz's single rule for life, just as it had been his own up until ten months ago.

Right up until Brady had appeared in his life.

'When does it start, next week?' Oz had asked. And then, the killer question. 'Did you know that Flávia Maura is scheduled to be talking on Paulista's lecture programme?'

Even then, in that moment, something had kicked, sharp and unexpected, low in Jake's gut. He'd tried valiantly to ignore it, but now he knew that had been nothing compared the maelstrom tumbling around inside him now.

'You know who she is, don't you?' Oz had continued, oblivious. 'She worked on the chlorotoxin you're using in these trials for a while, though I read an article a few months ago that said she's now switched to working on a venom from some species of bushmaster viper that might be able to break down cancer cells without damaging healthy cells. I'd have thought it would have been right up your street. Isn't it a step on from this scorpion-venom-based toxin we're using here?'

'Yes, I know what it is,' Jake had bitten out at length.

Just as he'd known who Flávia was.

And yet, he'd stayed silent. Oz had had other ideas.

'So you've heard of this Flávia, then?'

There had been nothing else for it.

'As it happens, I caught a lecture of hers by accident a little while ago.'

'Really? Is she as wackadoodle as they say?'

There had been no reason for him to bristle on her behalf. No reason at all. And even now, half a world away from that OR and only metres away from Flávia, he felt…not *protectiveness*, obviously, but *something*…even more strongly.

'She's…quirky,' he had admitted reluctantly.

'Quirky? I guess that's one word for it.' Oz had snorted. 'But then, I suppose you have to have something different about you to want to work with an animal, or whatever, that could kill you in a matter of hours. And that's after it has induced vomiting and dizziness, severe internal bleeding and organs shutting down.'

'She loves what she does.' He had shrugged, remembering the passion in her voice as she'd talked about how important the snakes were, and how it was a shame that the only way she could save them from man was proving to man that the snakes could ultimately provide the key to curing cancer.

'And she's highly intelligent.'

'Right.'

'She's hot, too. I've seen a photo. Hence hoping I'd be in Brazil for their summer programme.'

He hadn't liked the way Oz had been eyeing him so astutely. His mate wasn't stupid, and one wrong answer would have given the game away. Jake had known he needed to watch what he'd said next, especially with the anaesthesiologist pretending to be preoccupied and the scrub nurses hanging off their conversation. At least it was a team he trusted.

But still.

'Didn't particularly notice.'

It hadn't been so much a lie, but more a whole tightening around his chest, as though the air was being squeezed out of his lungs. It was ridiculous, and yet he hadn't seemed able to stop it; this woman—this stranger—had such an effect on him.

The effect her presence was having on him even now.

Him.

Jake Cooper. Bowled over by a woman he hadn't even spoken to. Bowled over by *any* woman, full stop. It just didn't happen.

'Really?' Oz had looked sceptical. 'I'd have thought she'd have been just your type.'

'I didn't know I had a type.'

'Smart, stunning and single-minded when it comes to career? You've got a type, all right.'

'You mean as opposed to you.' Jake didn't know how he had managed to force the light, wry note into his tone. 'You just go for female, attractive and up for a good time.'

And Oz had laughed. As though it had been just another version of the conversation they'd been having for years.

'Nothing wrong with that. As long as we're all consenting adults and all that.'

'Yeah, well, I just attended her lecture. Don't really recall anything else.'

And if it was an outright lie, then Jake had consoled himself with the lie that at least he was the only one who had known.

Still, Oz had eyed him critically.

'Bull. I don't buy that. You definitely would have noticed her,' he had countered. 'Oh, wait, did you sleep with her and never tell me?'

Jake remembered the way the accusation had riled him. Odd, since it never had done in the past. And even then, as he'd scrabbled about for a deflection, he'd known he was in trouble. Even if he hadn't realised how deeply.

'Listen, that lecture was a couple of months after Helen's death. After Brady.'

At least that bit hadn't been a lie.

'Ah, say no more.' Oz had backed off instantly. 'How is the champ?'

Jake remembered pausing. Exhaling deeply. He hadn't liked using Brady to change the conversation like that, but at least there was something of a poetic truth to it. Plus, his nephew catapulting into his life as a seven-year-old orphan was when Oz had proved their friendship of almost a decade was built on more than just nights out after hard operations.

Not every best mate would have been thrilled with a seven-year-old kid bursting in on their bachelor lifestyles, but Oz—the oldest of four brothers—had taken it in his stride, able to relate to Brady in a way Jake himself still hadn't managed.

His nephew was still a complete mystery to him. And it shamed him, angered him and frustrated him, all at once. He wasn't a man accustomed to failure. He had never failed. At anything.

But he'd failed at being a brother to Helen and now he was failing at being an uncle, and sole guardian, to Brady.

And he hated himself for it.

'No idea how he's going to take to Brazil,' Jake had begun. Then, 'No idea how he's going to like it with only me to talk to.'

'You'll cope.'

If only he felt half as confident as Oz.

He could deal with tumours, dying patients, grieving families. But he was at a complete loss when it came to talking to one grieving seven-year-old boy.

'I suggested going to a water park when I have a free weekend,' he'd told his mate.

'And?'

'He agreed.' Jake grimaced at the memory just as he had done when recounting it to his friend.

'But he wasn't exactly jumping up and down like most seven-year-old kids would.'

'That's because Brady isn't most seven-year-olds.' Oz had shrugged, like it was obvious. 'Did you offer to take him into the rainforest? *That* would have him leaping around like a maniac. In fact, you'd probably get home to find he'd packed both your suitcases. They wouldn't contain anything you needed, of course, but he'd have his test tubes, his sample pots and his magnifying camera for every insect or arachnid you could possibly find.'

'I considered it. But you really think taking a young kid into the rainforest is a responsible thing to do? I couldn't guarantee keeping him safe.'

'*You* wouldn't,' Oz had scoffed. 'You and I are city guys through and through. But you can get guided tours, some especially geared up for kids.'

'How the hell do you know that?'

'Brady told me.' Oz had sounded surprised. 'He didn't tell you?'

No. He hadn't. Because the fact was that Brady barely exchanged a word with him, if he didn't have to. Which told him altogether too much about the kind of absent uncle he'd been—and he didn't like it.

'Okay, that's the next step done.' Oz had confirmed his focus squarely back on the patient—not that it had ever really left—and Jake was grateful for the change of topic. 'Just one more and you can finally show me this tumour paint close-up. Man, I'd have killed to get this clinical trial of yours.'

'What can I say? They only choose the best.'

'You'd think you'd won awards for your research or something...' Oz had stopped abruptly, his entire demeanour changing in an instant. 'Ah, wait, is that it?'

He'd moved aside to give Jake room.

'Kill the lights, please,' Jake had instructed, all trace of their former banter gone as they'd focused on the task in hand.

The operating room had turned eerily dark, with only the light from the monitors casting out around the area. Then he'd shone a near-infrared light over the patient's brain and a pink-purplish glow had lit up.

'That's it,' Jake had confirmed with satisfaction. 'That's the chlorotoxin we injected last night.'

The chlorotoxin that Flávia Maura had worked on.

The thought had rattled through Jake's brain before he could stop it, proving that, even before tonight, with the vision of her in front of him, the woman had been positively haunting him. And no matter how many times he told himself it was purely professional interest, a part of him knew there was more to it.

'It's lit the tumour up like Christmas lights in a grotto.' Oz had shaken his head. 'I've seen it on footage but never in person like this. She's quite the beauty.'

'Remarkable, isn't it?' Jake had concurred, staring at the tumour. 'The engineered toxin fluoresces every cancer cell, yet leaves every single healthy cell around dark.'

'My God, it shows me every last bit of the tumour which I'd need to remove without worrying about margins and without fear of leaving anything behind, causing a recurrence. The only question will be whether it also interferes with the centres of the lad's brain responsible for speech or motor control.'

'That's your call.' Jake had nodded. 'How about get it out so that my patient can get his life back.'

'Okay, you're ready for the brain mapping? Can we go ahead and wake the patient, please?'

For the next hour or so, Jake had worked with the neurologist, using flash cards, asking questions and just generally keeping his patient talking whilst Oz had sent light electrical currents down the nerves to stimulate each part of the brain, then worked on removing the tumour.

And then Oz had given the signal that it was time to anaesthetise the patient again so that they could close up.

'Okay, mate,' Jake had told his patient. 'Next time you wake up, you'll be out of surgery.'

'You'll be with me?' the lad had managed.

'I'll come and see you as soon as I can and we'll talk you through how it's all gone,' Jake had confirmed, moving back to allow the anaesthetist to take over.

'Want to see?' Oz had offered when he was confident the lad was out again, but Jake had already been making his way around the table.

'I don't see any fluoresced areas.' He'd frowned in disbelief. 'You were actually able to get all of it?'

'Every last bit.' Triumph had reverberated through his mate's voice. 'Your patient might have to relearn his grade-two flute from when he was a kid, but if any tumour recurs in this guy, then it won't be because of anything I had to leave behind. You need to complete these clinical trials so we can get our hands on this stuff for every patient.'

'I'm working on it,' Jake had replied grimly. 'You know how long these things take.'

'Yeah, too long, when we've got patients to try to save. You'd better ask Ms Maura what else she has up her sleeve. And how long.'

And he'd filed it away as though professional interest was the only reason he was planning on talking to Flávia Maura.

They'd worked carefully, precisely, for a little longer.

'Now bone flap.'

Using plates and wires, they had secured the segment of skull they had removed in order to access the patient's brain. And then the surgery had been completed, and Flávia Maura had still been in residence in Jake's head.

'Nice,' Jake had congratulated as he and Oz left the OR together, trying to shake her, though not too hard. 'Good going.'

'Yeah, well, when you see the delectable Ms Maura, don't go doing anything I wouldn't do.'

'Apart from the fact that leaves pretty much everything on the table—' Jake remembered ignoring the jolt of anticipation which shot through him '—Brady will be with me. So my interactions will be strictly professional.'

Yet now, only three days later, and watching the woman agitatedly shift her weight from one foot to the other before finally taking her leave from the other women, he realised that his intentions towards Flávia Maura were far from strictly professional.

This he admitted as he strode forward and cut a slick path through the crowd to Isabella Sanchez—the woman running the gala evening's slick operation.

* * *

Three more nights, Flávia Maura chanted silently to herself as she took her leave from her colleagues, Doctors Krysta Simpson and Amy Woodell, and edged her way through the crowded ballroom with something approaching relief.

Three more nights of awkward social hospital events and then she could be out of the city and back to the rainforest, where she felt most at home.

It wasn't that she didn't like Krysta or Amy— far from it. She admired both women, who were incredibly accomplished in their careers and who seemed as kind as they were successful. She'd simply never been very good with crowds.

Animals were fine, but people…? Not so much. In fact, not only had her six- and nine-year-old nieces spent the previous weekend trying to give her a crash course in superficial conversation, but their mother—her own sister—had spent two hours this afternoon primping and preening her like some fun pet project.

Typical bossy Maria, Flávia thought fondly even as she anxiously tried to keep her balance in the unfamiliar skyscraper heels, and smoothed down her long gown. Her sister had practically bullied her into this dress tonight, and although it would undoubtedly look sleek and sophisticated on any other woman, it was all such a far cry from her usual uniform of trusty hiking boots and sensible, light grey cargo pants with a black tee that she felt like she might as well have been wearing little more than a scantily clad, samba carnival dancer.

Either that or like a little girl trying on her mother's clothes and high heels and lipstick, as her nieces had taken to doing with Maria's clothes. Flávia grinned to herself at the image of them playing princesses, even as an uncharacteristically melancholic pang shot through her. She loved the two little girls with all her heart, but sometimes—just occasionally—their lives reminded her of all that she and Maria had missed in their own childhoods. Not least the fact that their own mother had never stuck around long enough to give the sisters time to grow up and start to play dress-up in *her* clothes.

No. Their beloved *papai*, Eduardo, had raised them single-handedly, usually under the canopy of the Amazon or Atlantic rainforests, with explorer clothes instead of princess gowns, and animals for company rather than people. And Flávia had never regretted a moment of it.

Except when it came to taking life lessons from her nieces and then walking in on her sister stuffing condoms into her purse just before the taxi had arrived this evening, with an encouraging,

If you meet a cute doctor, why not try having a little fun for once in your life, Livvy?

But she didn't want to *have a little fun*. She was here because her boss demanded it, not because she had any desire to be; the sooner the night was over, the better.

She'd take a deadly bushmaster viper, a Brazilian wandering spider or a poison dart frog over trying to make conversation with a normal human being any day of the week. So between the hospital's packed social calendars, it was proving to be a particularly tense week.

Still moving—or rather, teetering—Flávia desperately scanned the ballroom, telling herself that she didn't need an escape route but searching for one all the same. Before her eyes alighted on the doors at the far end and a sense of consolation poured through her.

The botanical gardens were quite busy during the day, but at this time of evening they would probably be closed. If she could sneak in, it would give her a much-needed chance to regroup, and to quell the unfamiliar sensation of champagne bubbles up her nose from the glass she'd been trying to drink for the past hour.

She turned direction sharply, almost straight into one of her least favourite surgeons.

'The hospital should be more careful of their reputation,' the condescending tones of Dr Silvio

Delgado—clearly pitched to be heard by as many luminaries as possible, as though by denigrating everyone else he somehow elevated himself—reached her ears. 'First they hire the crazy *selvagem* woman, then the gigolo, and to add insult to injury, they then bring some frump in to lecture. This one looks like a street person.'

A better person, a stronger person, would have carried on walking, not letting that interminably pompous man get under their skin. But Flávia froze, shame momentarily rendering her immobile before eventually allowing her to twist herself around uncomfortably, a scowl pulling her features taut despite her best efforts not to react.

Selvagem—jungle woman.

It wasn't the term itself—she'd been called *selvagem* plenty of times and it didn't usually bother her—so much as the utter contempt in this particular man's tone. The pejorative way he spat out the word—*selvagem*—as if she was as feral as the animals found in the rainforest. Or was that just because Delgado had said as much to her face, many times in the past?

Perhaps that was why Flávia tried telling herself it was the fact that he was also insulting a new colleague—a visitor to Paulista's—which rattled her most.

Frump.

As though what Krysta wore mattered more

than the fact that the woman was a focused, driven individual, already a leader in the combined fields of otolaryngology and facial reconstruction.

Flávia felt as though she ought to say something. She wished she could. Then again, what was to be gained from drawing attention to something half the crowd mercifully hadn't understood, anyway, given that Delgado had spoken in Portuguese? Anyway, he'd only laugh her off, and she would probably let him.

All the more reason to get to the gardens and be alone.

Flávia gritted her teeth and gingerly lifted her foot, hoping she wasn't about to do something as stupid as catching the heel in the hem.

'Is that guy always such an abhorrent boor?'

Perhaps it was the clear-cut English accent which gave away the fact that the speaker was Dr Jacob Cooper. Or it could have been the rich, utterly masculine timbre, suggesting a barely restrained dynamism. Or maybe it was the fact that she remembered that voice only too well. It had featured in her pitiful dreams several times over the past eight months—and in those it wasn't just asking that one question after her lecture.

Whatever the truth, sensations skittered this way and that, like interlopers, inside Flávia's chest. The mere sound of his voice ignited every inch of her nerve endings, leaving her feeling as though her entire body was…*itching. On fire.*

An effect that no one had ever had on her before. Not even Enrico, the man who she had once called her fiancé.

Holding herself steady, Flávia spun slowly back around to face the speaker.

And promptly wished she hadn't.

CHAPTER TWO

THE MAN WAS—her brain faltered, flailing to understand what her eyes were seeing—simply extraordinary.

Last time she'd seen him, he'd been one figure in a sea of faces, every one of them clad in work suits, and yet, to her, he'd stood out. Now, he wore the same impeccable tuxedo as every other man. His hair the same, neat style as every other man. He was well groomed, with intelligent eyes the same blue as roughly three hundred million other human beings in the world. And yet…he wasn't the same as them.

There was nothing *the same* about Jacob Cooper, whatsoever. Indeed, far from her memory making more of the man than had ever really been, Flávia now realised, to her horror, that her brain hadn't *nearly* recalled quite how magnetic he was.

Flávia couldn't quite put her finger on it and yet it was there, nonetheless. Maybe it was that he seemed infinitely leaner, taller, more powerful, than any other man she'd ever known. Perhaps it was the way those eyes—as blue as a morpho butterfly—rooted her to the wooden dance floor.

And yet simultaneously made her feel as though she was floating a good foot or so above it. Or possibly, it was the fact that the air around her seemed to be heating up, as if flowing right from this stranger's body straight into hers.

Like nothing she'd ever experienced before.

She eyed the empty champagne glass accusingly. Evidently, the alcohol had allowed her sister's ridiculous *have a little fun* instruction to get into her head, and now it was running riot, upending the customarily neatly arranged compartments in her brain.

Vaguely, she recalled that he'd levelled a question at her, although for the life of her she couldn't remember what that question had been.

Her mind spun, the cogs slipping in their haste. *Ah, something to do with Delgado being a boor.*

She really ought to speak, but how could her brain form words when it couldn't even think straight? Flávia slid a discreet tongue over her teeth, unsticking them from her suddenly parched lips, and forced her vocal cords back into operation. And if her tone was a touch huskier than usual, well, was he really to know? From one lecture?

'You speak Portuguese?'

'A little.'

'That's unusual.'

He didn't so much as shrug to give the semblance of it.

'I made it my business to learn the language when I got the invitation to this summer's teaching programme and I knew that your man over there was head of the oncology department.'

Interesting.

'Why do that?' she couldn't help but ask. 'There are so many countries attending these annual summer teaching programmes that the common language is generally English, anyway.'

For a moment she wasn't sure he was going to answer her. His eyes bored into her and she felt something unfurl from her toes right the way up. Then, suddenly, he spoke.

'Let's just say that I make it my business to understand the nature of the people with whom I'll be working closely over the next few months. I like to know their character and I like to know their mettle.'

He smiled. Or, at least, he bared his teeth into something which could equally have been a smile, or a grimace. And Flávia couldn't have said why it made her think that she pitied anyone who tried to stir things up with this man.

It also made her more open with him than she might otherwise have intended.

'Dr Silvio Delgado's grandfather was one of the founding contributors to this hospital.' As the man was all too fond of telling people at every opportunity. 'He believes that gives him an inalienable right to insult whoever he pleases.'

Like calling her 'jungle woman' and turning it into an insult.

Then again, was it surprising she was sensitive to it? A childhood of being mocked by the other kids—her sister leaping in to fight her battles—had left more of a scar than Flávia would have liked. Yet she suspected, right at this moment, that it was the idea of *Jacob Cooper* thinking she was a bit...*odd* that bothered her more than anything that idiot Delgado could ever say.

'Indeed,' he offered in a tone so neutral that Flávia couldn't ascertain anything from it.

It irritated her that she was trying.

Why should she care what this stranger thought?

'Jacob Cooper,' he introduced himself, his words like the sweetest caramel moving through her veins.

'Yes, of course.'

'Of course?' he echoed, a hint of a smile toying with his altogether too-mesmerising mouth. 'I didn't think we'd met.'

Flávia blinked, heat rushing to her cheeks. She could only hope that her colouring, and the light levels, concealed her embarrassment.

'Well, I mean...*of course* I know the name. After all, who, with any connection to the oncology world, doesn't?' She was babbling, but for the life of herself she couldn't stop. 'Dr Jacob Cooper…that is, *you*…have a reputation for pushing boundaries. Running clinical trials that others were too afraid to touch, like the scorpion-venom-based fluorescent dye which lights up cancer cells like some kind of personal beacon. Making Hail Marys look like a proverbial walk in the park.'

Oh, Lord, now she sounded like she was fangirling. *This* was why she hated people. She really had no idea how to talk to them without coming across as either aloof, or a bit of a fool. A *bobo*.

'Well, I'm flattered.' His voice sounded all the richer, and more luxurious, and Flávia wasn't sure she cared for the effect it was having on her.

Turning her into even more of an *idiota*.

She didn't want to shake his hand. She feared what that contact might do to her given the effect the mere sight of him had. Yet she watched her arm reach out nonetheless, as if under some form of energy other than her own muscles.

When he enveloped her not-exactly-petite hand in his much bigger one, making it seem more delicate than it ever had before in her life, her heart stopped. Hanging there for a beat, or ten—sensations raining down on her like she'd charged into the ocean splashing spray high into the air and was letting it land on her skin—before pounding back into life like a thousand horses galloping in her chest.

'Flávia Maura,' she bit out by way of introduction. And only after what felt like an eternity.

His eyes glinted, but still she couldn't read them.

'I know,' he answered evenly. 'If we're going for a mutual love-in, then I feel duty-bound to point out that you're one of today's foremost authorities in the field of venom-based medicine. I caught your lecture on the application of a cancer-targeting toxin in Brazilian wasp venom some months ago.'

'Oh…' she offered, hoping that her scorching cheeks didn't give her away. 'Right.'

She could hardly admit that she recognised him from one question out of the raft of them she'd had that day, could she? Hardly tell him that his face had invaded her dreams ever since, like she was exactly the kind of weirdo Silvio Delgado would love the world to believe. Hardly confess that she'd looked for him after that lecture, wanting to ask *him* questions of her own.

So, instead, she fell back on her usual safety net. Discussing facts like they were the only conversation she knew how to have.

'Polybia-MP1. It exploits the unusual make-up of lipids and fats within cancer-cell membranes and essentially creates holes in the latter. These gaps can be wide enough to let molecules like proteins escape, and since the cancer cells can't function without them, the toxin ultimately acts as an anticancer therapy.'

She stopped abruptly, aware that this time his mouth was more than twitching with amusement.

'As I said. I caught the whole lecture.'

'Yes…well…there you go.'

With more effort than she cared to admit, Flávia attempted to propel herself forward again, away from this mesmerising man, needing the quiet respite now more than ever.

'So what are you working on now?'

She stopped.

'I… Well… I'm pretty much living my dream. Working as a naturalist and researcher, splitting my time between caring for pit vipers in a sanctuary in the rainforest, and my work at Paulista's.'

'I heard you were looking for ways to use venom to halt the metastasising of cancer cells in humans? Amazing to think that what had started as a passion for the wildlife of the Amazon rainforest can now enable you to save human and snake lives, alike.'

Flávia froze, her body practically shaking.

'You've read my recent interview?' Her voice cracked with shock.

'Indeed.'

'In Portuguese,' she added weakly.

That slow, sexy grin of his was going to be her undoing. She was sure of it.

'So I noticed.'

It stood to reason that he would know of VenomSci's work. But the fact that he'd read a piece on her life, and her naturalist goals, *and then quoted them back at her*…? Well, that was doing insane things to her insides.

She needed to get away. *Now.* Before she did something as ridiculous as her sister had suggested.

Turning sharply, Flávia lurched off. It was only when she was a metre or so away that she realised he was falling into step beside her.

'Where are we heading?'

'We?' she managed. '*We* are not heading anywhere. *I* was heading to the gardens.'

He moved with an enviable ease and confidence. A self-awareness as though he expected people—the world—to make way for him. Then again, it probably did, given the way people were hastily repositioning themselves to make way for him.

'That desperate to escape already, huh?' His voice actually seemed to rumble through her. 'Well, sorry to be the bearer of bad news, but the gardens are locked now.'

'They are?' She snapped her head around. 'How do you know?'

He hesitated. So fleeting that anyone else may not have noticed it. But Flávia wasn't *anybody*. She hadn't avoided being bitten by the fast, deadly vipers she had come to love by failing to miss tiny, telltale signs. It piqued her curiosity in an instant, although Jacob had apparently already shrugged the moment off.

'I tried earlier,' he answered smoothly. 'They told me it was closed for the night.'

'I see.'

There was something else. Something more. She'd lay a bet on it.

'May I recommend the bar instead? That far end looks pretty quiet.'

She ought to decline.

Her mind was still racing. Trying to fill in that missing moment. And then she shocked herself again by flashing a dazzling smile, which her sister was always telling her to use more often with people other than merely her beloved nieces.

'Why not? I'm sure we can have quite the party of our own.'

She ought to tell him she wasn't interested in a party *of their own*. She ought to be mingling, the way her boss had told her to do. She ought to draw more people into the conversation—she could see a couple of other medical and surgical oncology team members hovering for a chance to talk to the highly respected Dr Cooper.

Yet she didn't say any of those things, and by the time she reached the bar, Flávia found herself alone with a man who made her body fizz disconcertingly, and an empty countertop.

Then, with nothing more discernible than a diplomatic hand gesture, two fresh drinks materialised in front of them. A glass of champagne for her and, she hazarded a guess from the deep amber colour of the liquid swirling in the tumbler, a top-drawer whiskey or cognac for him. And suddenly, inexplicably, it all felt slightly too... intimate.

Flávia opened her mouth to refuse the drink and take her leave—not that she really believed her single glass of champagne was to blame for this...*thing* that hummed between them, but why take any chances? And then he thanked the bartender.

She had no idea what it was about the simple gesture, so understated yet so polite, and so unlike too many of the doctors in this room who thought themselves too good for something as apparently irrelevant as good manners.

She turned her head to look at him again and, once again, her heart slammed into her chest for no apparent reason. Was breath truly seeping from her lungs like a popped balloon or was she just imagining it? And never mind the dress feeling constricting and small, right now it was her very skin which seemed to be too tight for her own body.

Flávia couldn't help it—her eyes scanned over him. Quickly. Then slowly. Like they didn't know where to start. Or maybe where to stop. And still she stood there. Still. Ensnared.

No man had ever got under her skin like this. Ever. She told herself it meant nothing. That she must just be feeling out of her depth at this welcome gala, and vulnerable after Delgado's dig.

'Dr Cooper—' she began.

'Jacob,' he interjected.

She sucked in a breath. 'Jacob,' she began, then paused. As ridiculous as it was, his name sounded altogether too intimate on her tongue. She tried again. 'Jacob...'

'But you can call me Jake,' he interrupted, and this time she knew she didn't mistake the amused rumble in his tone. 'And for the record, you really shouldn't let oafs like Delgado get to you.'

'I don't,' she denied hotly, then cursed herself for sounding so defensive.

'I beg to differ. It was clear from the way you reacted that he had rattled you. And you have to know that's only going to encourage him all the more. Bullies like him thrive off making others feel small.'

'I'm well aware of that.' She bristled, despite

her attempts not to. 'But it was the doctor he called a frump who I was most concerned about.'

'Who? Krysta Simpson? I'm running a case with her at the moment... Actually, it would interest you—the patient has oral cancer and I'll be using the scorpion-venom-based fluorescent contrast agent when I remove the tumour in their jaw. But the point is, there's no need for you to worry about Krysta. She's more than secure enough in herself not to let such a comment get to her.'

Yes, that much was clear. Flávia couldn't help thinking that if she had a fraction of Krysta's confidence then she, too, could be wearing a dress which—if she had to be entirely honest—might not be the most flattering, but in which Krysta looked entirely comfortable.

What must it be like to be so cool and self-assured when chatting with these people?

Instead here she was, feeling utterly self-conscious in a figure-hugging dress and statement shoes, both of which her far more fashion-forward sister had insisted on foisting on her for tonight's event. Yet all Flávia could think was that one couldn't make a silk purse out of a sow's ear—and she most definitely felt like a sow's ear. And no matter the shocked compliments she'd been receiving all night.

Hastily, she told herself that she felt nothing at Jacob's... Jake's...apparent appreciation. Assuming that was what this was, of course. And if he did appreciate her, then it was the dress he admired—her *sister's* dress—not *her*, per se.

Only, she wasn't sure she believed that. Or, more pertinently, *wanted* to believe it.

Admittedly, she adored the colour—a forest green which shimmered to inky black as she moved, the stunning colour so like another of her beloved snakes—but other than that, she was too plagued with self-doubt to relax. Was the neckline too low? The slit in the skirt too high? Did it cling to her a little too much when she moved?

Her only consolation was that if she *had* looked as *on display* as she'd feared, then Silvio Delgado would surely have taken great delight in mocking her clothes, as well as her choice of career.

So maybe it was more that the clothes mirrored her environment and how she felt about her state of mind? Out in the forest, in her bush gear, she felt strong, powerful, in control. She spent practically twenty-three hours out of twenty-four in blissful solitude, with the glorious orchestra of the rainforest pleasing her senses. Here in this ballroom, in this city, harsh sounds assailed her from every side.

Some people loved the city with its shimmering lights, vibrant sounds and bustling life—her sister and brother-in-law being prime examples—but Flávia had never been able to understand its allure. Whether it was the light pollution, the noise pollution, the air pollution, Flávia couldn't be sure.

She felt out of her depth, like she was suffocating.

At least, she *had* felt that way, right up until a few minutes ago—ever since Jacob Cooper. Now, the butterflies were still there, but instead of flutterings of fear and discomfort, she could swear they were flutterings of...awareness? Anticipation? Not least because he was looking at her as though he thought she was the only woman in the room.

And then she hated herself, because her goosebumping body seemed to find that rather too thrilling.

'Did you want to speak to me about anything in particular?' The question came out sharper than she'd intended.

'Frankly, Flávia Maura, I find myself curious about many things right now,' he answered, and she couldn't have said why but she wasn't sure he'd intended it to have quite the huskiness that it did. 'But how about we start with your antivenom therapy, and how you think your snakes can change the face of cancer treatment today?'

She could see the inherent danger in responding to Jake's question—the effect he was having on her just from a few minutes in his company.

Yet, like a frog attracted to the sweet-scented nectar in a tropical pitcher plant, Flávia couldn't resist the open invitation to talk about her work— her true passion.

Even as she knew that, like the pitcher plant, a man like Jake would eat her up in a heartbeat.

Worse, the naughtiness of such an idea was almost deliciously thrilling.

She shook her head. It didn't completely rid her head of the uninvited images, and that made her feel more combative than she knew she should.

'You say it as though I'm suggesting the awful hoax remedies they call "snake oil."'

'On the contrary,' Jake answered easily. 'I'm well aware of the difference between "snake oil" and very real medicine. A recent study listed six groups of venom-based drugs which have gained FDA approval in the last thirty-five to forty years.'

Flávia didn't know whether to be impressed by his knowledge or irritated that it wasn't helping her to be any less attracted to him. She gritted her teeth.

'I'm guessing that you also know that captopril, an ACE inhibitor used to treat high blood pressure, some types of congestive heart failure and kidney problems caused by diabetes, is derived from snake venom?'

'I do know that, given that it's used by around forty million people worldwide.' Jake nodded.

'Well, did you know that it comes from *bothrops jararaca*, which is another of the Brazilian pit vipers I deal with?'

'That part I didn't know,' he conceded, and Flávia didn't like that it gave her such a punch of triumph.

Was she really trying to impress this man that much?

'Plus, clinical testing for venom-based drugs began in 1968 with an anticoagulant derived from a Malayan pit viper venom.'

'I didn't know that, either,' he acknowledged with a grin that revealed straight, white teeth. As though he knew exactly what she was trying to do.

'So, *jungle woman*,' he asked softly in a way that didn't make the term sound like an insult whatsoever, 'what makes pit vipers so special?'

'Because of disintegrins,' she declared firmly, unable to help herself. 'Which is a group of proteins found in bushmaster venom. Furthermore…'

The low reverberation of a gong cut her words short, and Flávia spun around as Isabella stepped forward to announce that the dinner was about to be served.

'Shall we?'

Dropping her eyes, Flávia took in the sight of

Jake's proffered arm and strove unsuccessfully to quash another bout of shimmering nerves.

She bit back the stuttering words which suddenly cluttered up her throat and swallowed once, *twice*, until she was sure she could answer with confidence, even if she didn't feel it.

'I don't believe we're sitting at the same table so you should probably ask one of the women at your table. There's a seating chart by the entrance.'

'Actually, I believe we are.' His voice rumbled around her, skimming over her skin and making it prickle like she'd somehow missed a joke she hadn't realised someone had told.

'Oh. Right.' Her voice sounded odd, but she couldn't help that.

It was the way he was watching her so curiously. So intently. His eyes holding hers and preventing her from dragging her gaze away, however hard she tried. And she did try. Because the longer he held the contact, the more certain she was that he could see into her, far deeper than her mere soul. Right down to that dark, unwelcome pit inside her, and every embarrassing secret that she'd long since buried within.

'Very well, then.'

Squaring her shoulders, Flávia raised her arm and linked with Jake, but still she couldn't steel herself enough against the thrill that rippled through her at the contact.

It was only as they moved to the entrance and past the board that she sneaked a glance at the chart; as she'd suspected, Jake—it still felt odd not thinking of him as Dr Jacob Cooper—wasn't supposed to be at her table. Yet when he walked her to her seat—through the round tables, with their pale damask cloths and stunning flower-covered topiaries—there was his name, at the place setting right next to hers.

And she was far too pleased about it for her own liking. Not that she had to let him see that. She pulled her face into a disapproving frown.

'Did you sneak in here and change this around?'

'Are you accusing me of schoolboy tactics?'

Another grin, and another glimpse of that perfect mouth, which she couldn't stop imagining against her skin. At the hollow of her neck, or trailing down her body. This time, there was no pushing the images away. So, instead, she focused on the rules. The regulations. The things which couldn't get her into trouble.

'You can't just move things around on a whim. How did you even get in here? You realise these doors were locked for a reason?' She was rattling off too many questions, but she couldn't seem to stop herself. 'Months and months of planning went into this. Besides, you're meant to be on one of the VIP tables, with Silvio Delgado. Experts in your field. How do you think he's going to react to someone from my table being bumped up to take your place at his table?'

Despite her rambling, Jake looked as composed as ever. He flashed her another even smile, and Flávia told herself she didn't feel it rushing through her, right down to her very toes. The thing was, no matter how Dr Delgado reacted to Jake's stunt, she couldn't imagine it intimidating the man standing in front of her right now.

Honestly, she couldn't imagine *anyone* intimidating this man.

'I imagine Silvio will be rather irked.' Jake shrugged, proving the point. 'But then, I imagine if it wasn't me inconveniencing him, then it would be someone else, so that's no great issue. Besides, do you not think that you're as much an expert in your field as he is in his, Flávia?'

'Yes, well…' Heat flushed her at the compliment. 'You still can't go around moving people *quer queira ou não.*'

'I don't see why not.' He laughed, a deep, rich sound which…*did things* to her.

'Dr—'

'Fine.' He cut her off with another dazzling smile. 'Would it settle you to know that *I* didn't change the place settings?'

'Really?' Flávia raised her eyebrows sceptically. 'Then who did?'

'Isabella Sanchez,' he answered slowly, flicking his arm out to where Isabella was leading another guest—presumably the guest originally intended to sit at their table—to Silvio Delgado's table—as if playing his trump card.

Then again, he *was* playing it.

Isabella was ultimately responsible for organising this entire programme. She wasn't a surgeon, or even a doctor, but she practically ran Hospital Universitário Paulista single-handedly. There wasn't a single thing which went on within the brick, glass and metal walls that Isabella didn't know about, and she controlled the floors with an iron fist clad in the most silken, smooth glove. She truly was a woman so formidable that even Silvio Delgado would be taking his life into his hands going up against her.

'Why would she do that?' Flávia shook her head.

'Because I asked her to.'

'Why?'

It still didn't seem to make any sense.

'Because I wanted to meet you properly.' He lowered his voice until she had to lean in to hear him, so that she was no longer sure if they were talking medicine, or not, and it suddenly felt entirely too intimate.

'I wanted a chance to talk to you.'

Flávia didn't answer.

She couldn't.

For the longest time she just watched him, his eyes snagging hers and refusing to let her look away. And she had the oddest sense that she was telling him entirely too much even though she wasn't saying even a word. That he was reading the truths she preferred to keep securely hidden.

Oh, boy, she really was in so much trouble.

CHAPTER THREE

'But if a bite from these vipers could kill a human within hours, or even minutes,' a Spanish doctor was asking Flávia, 'surely you can't cure cancer by injecting the venom without killing them? Not unless you're reverse-engineering a synthetic version.'

Jake took a spoonful of his dessert, a velvety crème brûlée which he barely even tasted, and tried to work out what the hell he thought he was doing.

Flirting with Flávia Maura?

The way he'd been doing for the past two hours. From even before she'd turned her mesmerising eyes on him and her smooth, lilting voice, which could surely have charmed arboreal snakes from the trees, had wound through him like a boa around its prey.

Business, he reminded himself, savagely turning his attention back the conversation which had all the table joining in.

'Well, that all depends on the snake, the make-up of its venom and even its delivery method. And, of course, it also depends on what we're trying to achieve.' Flávia leaned forward.

There was no doubting that her career truly drove her on, and he couldn't help but find it an exceptionally attractive quality. She was even more focused than he was—which was saying something.

'You'll know, I'm sure, that snake venom is a cocktail of hundreds of different components, including minerals and proteins, peptides and enzymes,' continued Flávia. 'Our goal is to isolate and then repurpose certain toxins within this venom, which would ultimately kill cancer cells whilst leaving healthy cells intact.

'There's an Australian researcher, Pouliot, who has been working on venom which will stop metastasis in breast cancer. He has been able to reverse-engineer venom from *bothrops alternatus*, which is a different bushmaster to the one I work with, and lab clone an inhibitor. However, he has still been unable to reverse-engineer and clone an inhibitor from the *microvipera lebtina*, so for that study he still needs live venom on hand.'

'Given how aggressive these deadly serpents are, you must be more than keen to reverse-engineer it to isolate and lab clone the toxins you need,' another of the diners declared. 'So that you won't need live snakes so much any more.'

Jake found himself pausing, his spoon halfway to his mouth. Was it only him who noticed the way her body stiffened ever so slightly? The way her back pulled that little bit tenser?

And then Flávia turned that hot, caramel gaze on him and his whole body kicked up a notch.

Business, he roared silently again. *Not pleasure*.

He suspected he was fighting a losing battle.

Twelve months ago, he would have willingly blended the two. If the chemistry that arced and sparked between them was anything to go off, he could only imagine how glorious the sex would be. Although his mind was doing a sterling job of painting a picture.

Grinding his teeth together, Jake shook his head, as if that could somehow free his mind from the grip of too many deliciously tempting images. But as he'd told Oz—was it really only three days ago?—that wasn't who he was. Not any more.

Not since Helen's death, and Brady's appearance. Not since this whole past horrific year.

'Actually, quite the opposite.'

He was vaguely aware of Flávia's response. Albeit through a slight haze.

'Bushmasters are actually very gentle, sensitive and fragile animals. If you approach them correctly, then they rarely harm. But their backs are like glass, and if you don't handle them with care they can, quite literally, break their spines twisting away from you. It has always devastated me to think that in the herpetologist Raymond Ditmar's books from the 1920s and '30s, the suggested method of catching snakes was to noose them from a safe distance. But for the delicate bushmaster, this will actually snap their backbones.'

A couple of the diners frowned.

'Nonetheless,' one of them persisted, 'lab cloning must be preferable, on the basis that even mishandling the tiny pot of venom extracted from these vipers of yours could kill you, even by simply getting a splash on your skin.'

'Let me tell you a not-so-secret fact about me.' Flávia smiled, and Jake thought that perhaps it was only him who could tell that it was just a little too tight at the corners of her mouth to be as genuine and open as everyone else seemed to think. 'My whole reason for moving into the venom-therapy world of cancer cures was not to save humans, but to save snakes.'

'I don't follow?' another diner pressed, clearly as enthralled as the rest.

And who could blame them—he wasn't far behind them. For all his self-recriminations.

'Don't misunderstand me,' Flávia pressed on. 'I love the thought of being able to come up with a solution that halts the metastasis in cancers. But what *truly* drives me is the knowledge that the bushmasters and others are now listed as vulnerable, because as we humans decimate their natural habitats in the Atlantic Forest, their populations have plummeted.'

'Surely, all the more reason to reverse-engineer a synthetic toxin?'

Flávia's smile brightened even further, and once again, Jake was convinced that only he felt its sharpness cutting through the air.

'Or perhaps an opportunity to educate people to take more care of these snakes. It might not be perfect that we have to prove these animals could save human lives in order for humans to start trying to save the animals in turn, but it's a good place to start.'

And it was in that moment that Jake grasped the depth of his peril. Because Flávia Maura and her obsession for her work was well and truly under his skin. Where it simply couldn't be.

Where he couldn't let it be.

He had no room in his life for anything but Brady and his career. Not that it was love—he knew that wasn't possible, though perhaps he might have better understood such an emotion if his own parents had set any kind of example of a caring, loving marriage. No, his parents had ensured that emotions weren't an affliction from which he was ever likely to suffer. But he had responsibilities nonetheless. Like work, and his nephew. He had to get them both back on track. This inconvenient attraction to Flávia Maura couldn't get in the way of that. It wouldn't. He refused to allow it.

'You look a million miles away.' Her gentle voice tugged him back into the room. And he had no idea for how long he'd been distracted, but her previously enraptured audience was now, finally, engaging in conversations of their own.

'Or are you only six thousand miles away?' she added. 'Back in London, perhaps? A girlfriend?'

What did it say about him that he was already searching her tone for something approaching... disappointment?

He shouldn't bite. It made no difference.

'No girlfriend.' He told himself he wasn't still searching for her reaction.

Good thing, too, since she kept her tone excruciatingly neutral.

'Ah. You just seemed distracted. Or bored.' Her expression pulled suddenly tight, and her cheeks flushed a dark pink. '*Meu Deus*, have I been rambling too much about the rainforest? Everyone tells me I do that.'

'No.' He reached to place his hand on hers before he could stop himself, his whole body jarring as though from a jolt of electricity at the contact. And by the way Flávia was staring down at it, her entire body now stiff, she was equally shocked. 'Absolutely not. Talking to you has been even more interesting than I had imagined it would be.'

He should stop there. Anything more wasn't her business. It wasn't *anybody's* business, ever. But especially not when they were at a table with ten of their colleagues, even if those colleagues were beginning to move around now that the meal was over, all engrossed in their own conversations.

'But… I really ought to go and check on something. Will you excuse me?'

Setting his napkin on the table, Jake stood abruptly. He really did need to go and check on Brady, even if it was just a phone call to Patricia, the retired nurse the hospital had engaged as a quasi nanny for this teaching programme, back in the accommodation the hospital had also provided.

Yet, more than that, Jake needed a reason to put a bit of distance between himself and Flávia Maura.

The woman was like no one else he'd ever met in his life, he thought as he strode across the room, deftly avoiding calls from other colleagues to come and join their conversations. The woman drew him in, slowly, inexorably, until suddenly he'd found himself about to tell her personal details he would never willingly share with anyone else; it was altogether too…*disquieting*.

He'd known he was attracted to her ever since he'd seen her give that lecture. But he hadn't been prepared for this. The way she made the air sparkle around her.

Around *him*.

If he'd thought her career drive and passion, her ability to shape the medical landscape with every project she undertook, was intriguing, then it was only exceeded by her captivating voice, her Delphian smile, her mesmerising body. Flávia Maura was utterly intoxicating.

And he was already captivated.

Reaching the lobby now, Jake slid his mobile out of his pocket. Once he'd ensured that Brady was all right, he would go back and find Flávia. He still had a plethora of questions for her, but this time he was prepared for her.

This time he wouldn't allow her to slide into his head.

'I was beginning to think you'd left.'

Flávia spun around with a low gasp. She'd thought she'd be alone here, in the botanical gardens, where no one else was likely to want to venture at this hour. Especially since, as Jake had told her earlier, they had indeed been locked up and she'd had to bribe the hotel's concierge to let her sneak in for a few moments.

Sometimes, it seemed, being the infamously mad *jungle woman* did have its merits.

'You startled me.'

'My apologies,' he offered. Only, he didn't seem remotely repentant.

Much the same way that he'd refused to apologise for having Isabella change the seating arrangements last minute.

She told herself not to feel so flattered.

'I've spoken to Isabella,' she told him before she could stop herself. 'She confirmed that you asked her to change the table plans for the sole reason of talking to me.'

'You needed confirmation?' He looked unperturbed, and she flushed slightly.

Still, she was determined to stand her ground.

'She also told me that you declined her offer to bump me up to your original table.'

He didn't answer, though he lifted his shoulders—yet somehow it was too gentlemanly to be a crude shrug.

'You didn't want Silvio Delgado causing a scene and making me feel uncomfortable.'

It was a stab in the dark, not even an educated guess, but when after the briefest pause Jake dipped his head, she knew she was right.

That he should have been so considerate to her

roared through her like a battle cry, screaming at her to fight this insane attraction to a man she barely knew.

Even if her years of following his work made it feel like otherwise.

'How did you know I was in here, anyway?' She tried to pull the conversation back onto safer ground.

'I've been looking for you for the past half hour when I remembered you were heading for here earlier to hide out after that first incident with Delgado. What are you doing in here alone?'

'I'm not hiding out,' she snapped, a little too sharply.

His mouth pulled at the corners and, too late, she realised he'd been baiting her and she'd fallen for it.

'Anyway, why were you looking for me? I thought you were meeting someone?'

It was such an obvious attempt to change the topic and yet, despite his attempt to give himself space and regroup, for some inexplicable reason Jake heard himself replying to Flávia.

'Not meeting, just checking on.'

'Doesn't sound remotely stalkerish.' She arched her eyebrows.

Although—even if she hadn't heard the stories about the perennial bachelor Jake Cooper—

she could never have imagined him chasing after any woman.

'I'll bear that in mind.' His tone was dry, but clearly he wasn't about to elaborate.

She told herself there was no reason to feel disappointed. Yet still, she did.

Well, what did you expect? she berated herself silently. *That wanting to talk shop with you over dinner meant you're suddenly the man's confidante?*

And then he shocked her by continuing.

'I went to check on Brady. My nephew. He's seven and he's being looked after by one of Paulista's retired paediatric nurses. Still, he's in a strange country and a strange room, and I didn't want him to wake up and be disorientated.'

She wasn't sure which part of the admission hit her hardest. There were plenty of stories about Jake Cooper the supersurgeon, and just as many about Jake Cooper the stag.

But there were absolutely none about Jake Cooper the doting uncle.

'You have a...nephew?' She blinked abruptly, and he paused, but then continued.

'Yes. My late sister's son.'

Flávia opened her mouth, then closed it again. She thought of her sister, and her brother-in-law. And then she thought of her young nieces. When she spoke again her tone wasn't shocked, or gushing. It was just as honest and sincere as she felt.

'I'm so sorry for your loss. Was it recent?'

It felt like a lifetime that she thought he wasn't going to engage with her. And then…he did.

'Ten months,' he bit out.

'Was it sudden?' she pressed gently. 'Or was there some warning? Not that it's ever enough.'

Another long beat of silence swirled around them before he answered. Each admission drawn out from him as though he didn't want to, but as though he couldn't stop himself. Because Jake wanted to talk? Or because he wanted to talk to *her*?

Flávia wasn't sure. She told herself it didn't matter either way.

'Oesophageal cancer,' he growled. 'Apparently, she went to her local hospital with stomach pains and they told her they suspected gallstones and sent her home telling her they'd send a follow-up appointment within weeks.'

She could hear the gruffness to his voice and she knew he was trying to eradicate it. Didn't it speak volumes about the man's compassion that he couldn't quite manage to do so?

'She told me she took painkillers and missed the appointment because Brady had some recital she couldn't miss. Something about being a single mum.'

'I can understand that,' Flávia murmured quietly.

'By the time things got so bad that she had to call an ambulance, they diagnosed advanced oesophageal cancer and she finally called me to come up from London. We weren't exactly close the last ten years, the odd phone call once or twice a year.' She could hear the bitter notes he was trying too hard to conceal, and her heart ached for him. 'But we led different lives. Anyway, by then there was nothing they could do but move her to a hospice. She died six days later. Ironic, wouldn't you say?'

She cocked her head, studying him.

'Why?' she asked at last, the infinite sadness in his voice seeming to draw some invisible band tight—almost too tight—around her chest. 'Because you think you should somehow have been able to save her?'

'I'm an oncologist.'

'Can you save everyone who walks through your door? Especially when they come to you so late?'

He didn't like it—she could tell even as she ignored the part of her brain wondering *how* she could tell.

'She was my sister,' he ground out. 'And she was the only parent that seven-year-old boy had. I should have been able to do…something.'

His voice cracked suddenly. Unexpectedly.

Flávia didn't think, she just moved. Closing the gap between them and placing her hand on his forearm as though it could somehow offer him a comfort that no words could. And even when he lowered his head stiffly and stared down at it, as if wondering where the contact had come from, she didn't move.

Neither did Jake.

'And now you're doing the only thing you can. You're his legal guardian.'

'Yeah.' His voice hardened to a grim, self-deprecating edge. 'Jake Cooper, the guy with the reputation as an emotionally detached work-aholic.'

'But clearly, your sister thought you were the right choice.'

'Not really. I was just the only choice Helen had.'

'I can't imagine…' Flávia trailed off. 'So your parents are…have passed away?'

The silence eked out between them. So long and so heavy that Flávia began to wonder if she could say something else until, finally, he spoke.

'This isn't a conversation you should be burdened with.' He was too clipped, too crisp.

Clearly, he didn't *want* to be having the conversation with her. But not wanting to and not *needing* to were two different things. That was something she knew for herself all too well.

'We should go back,' he rasped. Still not moving.

And Flávia didn't answer, yet it was disconcerting the way those deep, dark cacao depths of hers seemed to pierce right through him. It felt as if she could see right through to his very soul.

So she slid her hand gently down his arm, covering his hand with hers, and she waited for him to pull away and head for the door.

But he didn't move. And he didn't pull away.

'I have a sister,' Flávia murmured at last when she thought he'd passed up enough chances to shut things down for good. 'Her name is Maria, and she has two daughters. Julianna is nine and Marcie is six, and I love being the fun aunt. We've always been a close family.'

'I've never been the *fun* uncle.' She suspected that the words were out before he could bite them back.

'I can't even begin to think how I would feel if anything happened to any of them,' Flávia continued softly. 'I have an apartment in the city for when I'm not at the sanctuary. But most of the time I end up staying at their home, Maria and Luis's—that's my brother-in-law. Their guest room seems to have become my personal bedroom and I always get at least one of the girls sneaking in for a sleepover.'

She laughed and even to her own ears the love and warmth of the sound seemed to reverberate around the room. Like it was too big to be contained in this space.

Which was how it always felt to her.

However, Jake wasn't smiling. He was grimacing. He pulled his hand free and rubbed his eyes wearily.

'I'm pretty sure Brady couldn't care less whether I was around or not.'

'And yet, you just left this gala to make sure he was okay,' she pointed out.

'I made a phone call. I hardly dashed across the city.'

'Why even call, then?' she challenged softly, though a part of her already knew the answer.

He glowered at her for a moment before reluctantly conceding. 'I just wanted to call and make sure he hadn't woken up and panicked or become disoriented in the unfamiliar surroundings.'

'Does he often wake?'

'Pretty much never. At least, not any more.'

He didn't need to voice the words for her to imagine how different things would have been straight after his mother's death.

'And he hadn't woken tonight?'

'No.' Jake raked his hand through his hair in such a disarmingly boyish gesture. 'It seems Patricia has it all in hand.'

She couldn't pinpoint exactly why she sensed a slight undercurrent. She eyed him speculatively.

'Surely, that's a good thing?'

'Of course it is.' He bobbed his head as though the action could emphasise things even as his words failed to.

'Then why do you look as though something about it bothers you?' she pressed softly.

They were so close she could feel his breath on her cheek. Blowing over her eyelashes, and sizzling through her body.

An ache stole through her, settling in all the places it shouldn't. Heating her from the inside out.

Jake opened his mouth to tell her she was wrong, she was sure of it, but then he simply closed it again. Closing his eyes for a moment, like he was working out whether to answer or not.

'It doesn't bother me,' he denied eventually, his gaze snagging hers, and revealing all the things his lips were concealing.

Like the fact that his denial was a lie and there was nothing she could do about it. There was no way to help him. She didn't even understand why she so desperately wanted to. Or why she so badly wanted those lips to drop down to meet hers.

It made her feel out of control, and she told herself that couldn't be a good thing.

'I… I think I ought to head home.'

'During a welcome dinner?' He stopped abruptly and she told herself that it was fanciful to believe he was disappointed.

'The dinner is over,' she pointed out. 'I've done my duty. I've attended it and I've spoken to more people than I can remember tonight. I think I can safely sneak out without getting it in the neck from Isabella. Besides, I have a lecture to give soon. I can say I'm prepping for that.'

'You haven't prepared it?' One eyebrow rose in a perfect arch, and Flávia had to clench her hand in a fist not to reach up and trace the curve. 'I'd have thought you were the kind of person to have written it months ago, only needing to slip in new data as it emerged.'

Which was another way of saying he thought she was predictable, and nerdy. And though that was probably true, she suddenly, inexplicably, felt like doing something out of character. Something that would take this man, who seemed to think he had the measure of her, by surprise.

It made no sense, but Flávia didn't care. She told herself it was the wine talking, or her sister's well-intentioned advice, but deep down she knew neither were true.

And yet she found herself tilting her head back, meeting those piercing blue depths, and any last remaining voices in her head were silenced as she rolled up onto her toes and pressed her mouth to his.

Need punched through her in an instant—even before Jake angled his head and deepened the kiss. The slide of his tongue over hers making her blood tingle in her veins and a thrill zip around her body as his hands gripped her shoulders, pulling her in tighter.

She thought it would never end—she wished it could never end. Right up until the botanical gardens sprinkler system kicked into its nightly routine and showered them both. And even then, she didn't notice immediately.

It was the kind of fine downpour that looked as though it couldn't possibly even wet a leaf, but which ultimately soaked a person right through to the skin.

Flávia wasn't sure who broke the kiss first, her or Jake. She only knew that it had been with great reluctance. And that his hands were still holding her shoulders, just as hers were pressed against his chest.

One of them had to speak, even if she had no idea what to say next.

'So what now?' She choked out a half-nervous, half-amused laugh.

Deus, but she could so easily lose herself in those electric-blue pools of his when he looked at her like that.

'We are in a hotel,' he managed thickly, at last.

Her heart practically launched itself at her ribs, hammering so loudly it was impossible to believe he couldn't hear it. It was exciting. Thrilling. *Her*, the woman who hadn't had a fling in her life, taking her sister up on the teasing dare to *have a little fun.*

And with Jake she felt naughty, and daring, and not at all like her usual buttoned-down self.

The sense of freedom was heady.

'We are indeed,' she agreed, barely recognising the desire in her own voice.

This time, Jake didn't reply. Instead he took her hand, enveloped in his, and tucked her into his side as he hurried her across the floor and out of a hidden staff door to the side.

And all Flávia could do was follow. They were like two tree frogs hurrying to the shelter of a bark hollow to seek safety from a deluge.

CHAPTER FOUR

As THEY STEPPED through the bedroom door, Jake deliberately ignored that part of him demanding to know what the hell he thought he was playing at.

He had no idea how he'd managed to slow things down. He only knew that he needed to give her—and himself—time to think.

How had he let himself kiss her? More than that, when the sprinklers had started and they'd finally pulled apart, why had he decided the next best step was to usher her to the reception desk and book a suite upstairs for them?

As if he couldn't help himself. As if he hadn't risked any one of their colleagues walking out and seeing them. As if he wasn't now responsible to a little boy across the other side of town.

So much for not letting Flávia Maura slide under his skin.

He didn't know what had compelled him to book a suite for them, any more than he understood why he'd started to tell her things—like anything about Helen, and his irrational sense of guilt—that he'd never told anyone else in his life. Not even Oz.

Or, more to the point, he did know. He was just trying to pretend that he was still in control of himself—and not just the fact that he'd barely been able to keep his hands off her in the lift, enduring what had to be the longest elevator ride of his life.

This was the craziest thing he'd done in ten months—longer, really—and yet he couldn't bring himself to feel guilty. Was it really so much to crave one night with a woman who made him feel…*something* again? Was it too much to want to feel normal again, instead of feeling as though he was constantly on the brink of drowning in the responsibility of a seven-year-old boy who barely liked him, let alone wanted him around?

And, of course, Brady didn't want him. The poor kid just wanted his mother—and that was just one more thing for which Jake felt as though he'd failed his nephew.

Tonight.

One night.

With a woman who made him feel *alive*.

Closing the door behind them and leaning his head on the cool wood for a moment, he tried to make himself think. Only when he thought he finally had a grip on his uncharacteristically out-of-control libido did he finally turn.

Only to see Flávia clad in nothing more than the sexiest lace bra-and-panties set he could swear he'd ever seen in his life. And hold-ups, which practically stopped his heart in his chest. Her shimmering gown lay in a puddle around her sinfully high heels. Jake tried to force himself to think straight, but it wasn't easy when the woman had the kind of eyes that pinned him to the spot, the thickest and glossiest curtain of chestnut curls and a body which ought to be illegal, it was so dangerous.

There was no doubt about it: Flávia was some kind of goddess that no red-blooded male could ever hope to resist.

Or want to.

Yet for all that, her hands were clutched almost self-consciously to her front, over the apex of her slender, tanned legs that seemed to go on for ever and, despite his best intentions, made him imagine hooking them over this shoulders as he engaged in far more carnal pursuits.

A fresh lick of attraction wound its way over his body—hardly helping matters. Blood pooled in the hardest part of him. She made him feel hotter, greedier, more alive, than he'd ever felt in his life.

Worse, he didn't mind feeling so out of control—yet he surely should have minded.

Instead, all he could think of was how her skin would feel, right there in that inviting hollow of her neck, how those dark nipples—which were announcing themselves so proudly through the scrappy lace—might scrape the middle of his palms or under the pads of his thumbs, or how sweet she would taste if he crossed the room right now, lifted the hem of his tee and buried his face right there between those long, tanned thighs.

He snapped his eyes back up to hers, aware that he'd let them trail over her in a way to which she would no doubt object. But as those amber depths locked with his, his heart jolted. Because he didn't see censure, or displeasure, in her gaze; instead, he saw something far more primal. Something far more like a mirror.

The proof that, just like down in the gardens, she ached for him just as much. It was all he could do not to give in to this raw *need* which scraped away inside him. And then she pulled her lower lip in with her teeth.

'Is this…okay?'

It was incredible that she actually sounded uncertain. As if he might have, for some wholly ludicrous reason, changed his mind. Jake couldn't hold himself back any longer.

He closed the gap between them in an instant.

Fresh attraction arced between them, so bright and so electrifying that for a split second he was astounded that it didn't shock him where he stood. But then he was moving, gathering Flávia to him as he bent his mouth and tasted those honeyed lips for only the second time ever.

Yet as her body moulded all too willingly against his, Jake felt as if she'd been handcrafted just to fit him, and she was winding her arms around his neck as if hanging on for her life. And those small, needy sounds she was making in the back of her throat were doing nothing to help him regain any last scrap of self-control.

He'd put his life on hold for Brady for the past ten months, and he hadn't resented it even if he'd struggled to see how he was the best person for the task. And tomorrow he would go back to sacrificing for his nephew, because that was what Brady deserved.

But tonight?

Tonight was his. And Flávia's. To indulge and to be free. And he'd be damned if he wasn't going to enjoy every last second of it.

The instant before he claimed her mouth with his, Flávia had been telling herself that she was being silly. That practically stripping for the man was insane. That she needed to get back into her dress and get out of there and back home before she did anything else totally out of character.

But all of that had happened before Jake Cooper had lowered his head and taken her mouth, so purposefully and so expertly, with his own.

And suddenly she was on fire, and all she could do was try to match him, flame for flame.

She might not have taken Maria's suggestion to *have fun* seriously this afternoon, but she had every intention of following it to the letter right now. After all, when would she ever come across another guy like Jake, who had made her feel fluttery in her chest—and, all right, a damned sight lower—just from a first look?

Even after that horrid Silvio Delgado's *jungle woman* jibe. In fact, Jake had been the one to turn it around and make her feel as though the work she did was the *only* thing he was interested in, in a room full of top-flight medical colleagues.

No, she wasn't about to give him reason to suddenly wonder what he was doing up here with her now, when he could be with someone a little more cultured. So she gave herself up to every last sensation. Dancing in the flames of the same scalding hot desire that had been licking at her ever since that first moment in the bar. But now they weren't merely licking at her, they were consuming her.

And Flávia never wanted the fire to die down. She lifted her hands and flattened them against the solid wall of his chest, revelling in the hard ridges and contours which seemed so opposed and yet perfectly paired to her soft palms.

It wasn't mere heat. It was scorching. Tearing

right through her like a blaze through dry tinder. The slow drag of his mouth over hers, the decadent tease of his tongue, the gentle pull of his teeth on her plump lower lip.

She gave herself over to every second of it. Meeting him and matching him. When he was done, she felt almost bereft, but then he repeated it, a little faster this time, a little harder, a little naughtier.

And then again. Each time angling his head a different way, causing new sensations and leaving her begging for more. Over and over, as if he was every bit as lost in the moment, as incandescent, as she was.

It still wasn't enough. It should have scared her how much she wanted Jake, yet it didn't.

Instead, with every kiss she felt surer of herself, and of what she wanted, than ever before. He swept his hands up and down her spine, then to the sides, as though he was learning every contour. And taking his sweet time doing so. When she wasn't sure she could take any more, Flávia rolled onto the balls of her feet, lifting herself a fraction higher and pressing her body to his, moving a fraction closer. Wanting more but not knowing how to ask for it.

It was inexplicable.

She was hardly some untried virgin, but never had any of her few relationships ever made her feel this *urgent*, this *greedy*, this *wanton*. Not even Enrico. When Jake lifted up her arms to skim his fingers down her sides, her eyes locked with his and she revelled in the way his pupils darkened and his breathing sounded that little more ragged. Then he slowly, deliberately, lowered his head and took one upturned nipple deep into the heat of his mouth. Not even moving the fabric of her bra aside to do so.

Sensations exploded through Flávia.

Her back arched and she let her head fall back, losing herself in the magic of it. The way he toyed with her, teased her, sucking on her nipple, then grazing his teeth over it—pain and pleasure rolled into one. At some point, she realised he had deftly removed her bra, because when he lifted his mouth, cool air swirled around her nipple moments before he drew tiny whorls with his tongue. And all Flávia could do was gasp and run her fingers though his hair in a silent plea for him never to stop.

When he did, it was only to turn his attentions to her other breast, and repeat the whole glorious process all over again, those sensations in her core winding more and more taut. Fraught with need.

She had no idea how long they stayed like that, lost as she was in the moment. But suddenly he was lifting her up to wrap her legs around his waist, to nestle her softness against the hardest part of him, and as she heard the soft moan escape her lips she wondered how much longer she could hold out.

If at all.

'Bed,' Jake commanded brusquely, as if reading her mind.

She nodded, even as he was already on the move. Lifting her up and carrying her across the room like some kind of infinitely romantic gesture, before depositing her on the bed. She realised then that she was wearing nothing more than a skimpy metallic black scrap of material, whilst he was still in his full tuxedo.

She ought to feel embarrassed. She wasn't the kind of woman who had been especially comfortable parading around in front of her—albeit it two—serious boyfriends in such a scanty bit of lace. Yet with Jake she felt bold. Even naughty.

'I feel you're a little overdressed,' she managed huskily.

He looked down as if he hadn't even realised, then cast that rich gaze over her, all over again.

'Perhaps that's something you should remedy.'

An instruction, a command. And she'd never been so happy to obey.

Sitting up, she reached forward and hooked her fingers into his waistband, tugging him forward, not that he put up much resistance, and concentrated on undoing each button of his shirt. Her fingers actually shaking with anticipation as she pushed the sides open.

My God, he is glorious.

Hard ridges and sculpted contours drew her hands, and Flávia imagined she could spend a whole lifetime acquainting herself with the ever-delicious delineation. And another tasting it. She dipped her head and ran her tongue over one defined line and sensations burst in her mouth.

Salt and fire, and everything in between.

Jake.

She wanted more. As he concentrated on shucking off his top half, Flávia dipped her head and she traced more of him, learning the relief of his chest with her mouth and her hands, moving lower. And lower again. Until she was at the top of the deep V that led her tantalisingly down until it disappeared below the waistband of his trousers.

Her hands were shaking even more as she tried to work the zip, but she was determined not to let him see it. Not to let him realise how little experience she actually had. She had heard the rumours about Jake Cooper, and whilst he wasn't exactly a playboy, she knew he'd had at least a couple of high-profile…*partners* over the years.

For one night only, she was going to have that same kind of fun.

Pushing his trousers down with renewed confidence, she cradled his straining boxers and finally released him from his material cage. Yet nothing had quite prepared her for precisely how *impressive* the man was.

So hard, so velvety and so very, very hot. She wanted to touch him, to feel him, to *taste* him. But before she could do any of it, he was taking a step back.

'I don't have any protection,' he gritted out as though it was all only just occurring to him.

'Sorry…' Her head was swimming, not quite following.

'Condoms,' he bit out. 'I don't have any.'

Later, she would consider that it was a good sign that he hadn't been prepared for her or anyone else that night. Later. But not in that moment.

'In my clutch.' The words surfaced hazily. 'Over there.'

His eyes flickered but he turned with a harsh, 'Don't move.'

Not that she had any intention of moving.

'Do you always go around carrying so many condoms with you?' he demanded a few moments later as he unfolded them from the little purse like a magician producing ream after ream of coloured silk.

She flushed. 'Does it matter?

'Call it male ego,' he quipped, but she was sure there was an edge to his tone.

'My sister put them there,' Flávia managed.

'Ah…' His face cleared and, however fanciful it seemed, she felt it was like the sun coming out on a grey day.

'She might have been a touch overenthusiastic.'

'Yeah, well—' he discarded his remaining clothes and approached the bed '—I, for one, am pretty grateful right now.'

Anything else she might have said was chased from her head as he reached down and took her bottom, pulling it towards him until she was lying on her back, her hips raised whilst he removed the triangle of lace. And then he was alongside her, his mouth catching hers, demanding, and imprinting.

The kind of kiss her sister had waxed lyrical over but that she herself had never—until now—actually believed existed. It made her whole body sing. Soar. And when his hand skimmed over her belly, everything clenched and fizzled inside her.

He took his time, just like before. Only, this time, Flávia didn't think she could wait. She already knew the muscled chest, and the corded neck. She had acquainted herself with those strong arms. But now she needed more.

So much more.

Reaching down between them she took hold

of him, her fingers curling around his thickness. Surely, she had never felt anything so silken steel.

The man was incomparable.

'Slow down, *jungle woman*,' he teased, trailing kisses down her neck and to the sensitive hollow where she shivered with desire. But his voice was thick and, somehow, just like before, he made the name sound utterly sexy and not at all insulting when it dropped from his lips. 'I'm not sure I can hold out for long if you touch me like that.'

Flávia had no idea what took her over in that moment, yet suddenly she felt a boldness she'd never known before.

'That's what I'm counting on.'

A low, infinitely feral sound rumbled from his chest. Flávia felt it low in her belly. It pooled between her legs.

'Is that so?' he demanded gruffly, shifting position before she could answer.

Then his fingers were moving, travelling down her body. Over her stomach, and her lower abdomen, then lower still, until he was dancing long, clever fingers where the lace had recently covered, before dipping into her wet heat.

'Jake…' A whisper and an exaltation all at once. She arched her back, and moved against his hand.

'Patience,' he instructed, playing with her. Teasing her entrance, slowly at first, like he had all night and he intended to take his time. She wanted to tell him she needed more, but the words didn't materialise. Instead she moved against him, letting him build the rhythm inside her. A little faster now, dipping in once. Twice. Then returning to play with the core of her need.

And all the while, his lips were still paying homage to her mouth, her neck, her breasts. Like an exquisite assault from every direction.

She wasn't sure when it went from fire building to a blaze. It was as though it had been glowing for so long that she hadn't realised how close she was to combusting. Like starting a fire in the bush from a couple of sticks and a fluff of wool. One moment it's merely smouldering, and the next moment it's bursting into flames.

A yearning rushed her. Flávia shifted and jerked, raising up to meet his hand, knowing he was catapulting her to the edge and helpless to do anything but let him. She slid her hand up and under the pillows above her head. She was close. So close. And it was the most carnal thing she'd ever known. Then he flicked his wrist and slid two fingers inside her without letting up the pressure of his thumb caressing the centre of her need.

Flávia shattered.

She heard herself cry out, felt her whole body react, tensing, releasing and then tingling. From the top of her head right down to her toes, which were actually curling into the down cover, which they hadn't even bothered to remove.

Who knew that wasn't just a myth? she thought in wonder as she floated somewhere out there where no one had ever taken her before. She had no idea how long she stayed there, but when she came back to herself, Jake had moved. Settled over her, but propped up so that he wasn't crushing her.

She wanted to say something, but she couldn't. She could only take her hands from above her head and wind them around his neck, pulling him closer again. Right up until she felt him right *there*. Hot and ready, the hardest part of him against the softest part of her.

'Ready, Flávia?' he muttered, and for the first time she realised quite how hard Jake was fighting to stay in control.

It made her feel good. More than good.

'I don't know,' she teased. 'You might have to give me a bit longer to recover.'

'You don't have any longer,' he growled, and whatever else she was going to say to tease him was torn from her mouth as he flexed against her, his blunt tip nudging at her. A plethora of emotions cascaded through her all over again.

As he slid inside her, slowly and carefully at first, giving her a chance to shift, to accommodate him, a tenseness coiled itself around her belly again. So many sensations that she couldn't begin to identify them.

He began to move faster then. Sliding in, then out. Then in, and out. Stoking the fire that she now realised had only been lying dormant. She could barely move, barely even breathe. All she could do was wrap her legs around him, her fingers biting into those strong shoulders, and match him, stroke for incredible stroke.

Faster and deeper. Until she was grazing her hands down his back to clutch at him, and pull him in deeper.

'Flávia…' he groaned her name, her unexpected action making him jerk and thrust that little bit harder.

And sending Flávia that bit closer to the edge.

She repeated it with the same effect. All that bright sensation so close now she could almost touch it.

'Don't stop,' she muttered, her hands gripping him tightly, her bottom raising up to meet him, to match him.

She heard the guttural groan as he slid his way home for the last time, sending her soaring just like before.

And this time, when she fell off the edge, Jake went with her.

CHAPTER FIVE

'LIGHTS, PLEASE,' instructed Jake Cooper.

The operating room went dark, almost eerily so, with only the glow of the large operating monitors lighting up the space. And then Jake shone the near-infrared light over his patient's mouth.

One solid area glowed a purplish hue, with a tiny purplish dot slightly to the side. His patient's squamous cell carcinoma.

'There's our villain,' Jake announced to the gallery of residents watching this surgery to learn.

Once his team had removed it, along with part of the patient's jaw, he would pass the surgery on to Krysta Simpson, for her team to start reconstructing a new jaw based off a titanium plate.

All in all, it would be a circa ten-hour, multidisciplinary operation, but if he was honest with himself, he was relieved to be able to concentrate on something other than Flávia Maura.

Memories of that night had haunted him all week, and only his surgeries—demonstrating his clinical trial for residents and esteemed colleagues alike—gave him something else for his focus. So much for his promise to himself of one night, and then his entire focus would be on his responsibility for Brady.

He couldn't get Flávia out of his head. He even dreamed about her.

It was insanity.

Ejecting the thoughts from his head, Jake focused on the patient in front of him. It was an operation he'd performed many times in the past, but still he never stopped respecting what could happen with any patient on that operating table.

'That smaller dot there, that's where the tumour has started to metastasise?' one of the residents noted via the intercom from the gallery.

'Right.' Jake nodded. 'Too small to show up on any MRIs or CTs pre-op, if we didn't have the fluorescent contrast agent to light it up, we wouldn't have known it was there. We'd have resected assuming margins, and then had to wait for the pathology to come back to tell us if those margins were clear. At best, we'd have taken more than we needed, leaving our patient here with more of his jaw missing. At worst, we'd have taken too little and left some tumour in there, and we'd have only found out when the cancer recurred.'

'So that's it?' someone else asked. 'That tumour dye shows up exactly where the SCC is, and if we take everything that glows, we've got it? No need for margins?'

'That, ladies and gents, is what we're in this clinical study to determine,' Jake agreed. 'But so far, it's looking good. Anybody know what the national figures are for positive resections following surgery in head and neck squamous cell carcinomas?'

The intercom clicked a few times and then a female voice spoke.

'I read it was somewhere between fifteen and thirty percent with poor outcomes, ultimately necessitating some form or another of additional therapy.'

'Gold star, that woman,' Jake confirmed. 'So to combat that, we take greater margins and leave the patient with more disfigurement leading to a lowering of quality of life. Now, hopefully, we won't need to. We can see exactly what we're doing.'

'And leave the oral and maxillofacial reconstruction team with more to play with?' the female added.

'Right. We'll be doing a segmental mandibulectomy with a modified radical neck dissection on the left side of the mandibular structure. The reconstruction team are intending to use a plate reconstruction, so our goal is to leave them as much as possible.'

'Osseointegrated dental implants?' someone asked.

'Again, that'll be up to the OMS team. However, in this case, resection will likely result in significant loss of mandibular support to the teeth—though with this dye showing us exactly where the tumour is, we'll be able to really keep that to a minimum. Nevertheless, I think we can expect to lose all but one, maybe two molars, and a couple of root stumps, so conventional dental solutions will be unfeasible.'

Jake worked steadily for hours, careful to take all the tumour but leave as much healthy tissue as he could, and ensuring he stayed away from any major nerves which, if damaged, could leave the patient with facial paralysis, and finally he was on the last bit, and Krysta and her team were entering the OR ready for handover.

'How's it going?' Krysta asked.

'It's gone well,' Jake confirmed. 'We're completing a type-L modified neck dissection. The patient has remained stable throughout and there have been no complications. I've concentrated on areas here, and here, which is where the contrast agent highlighted areas outside of the normal scans.'

'Nice,' Krysta approved.

'I've left as much of the ascending ramus and condyle as possible.'

'Excellent.' She nodded. 'That gives me more than I was expecting to work with.'

Running through the remaining points, Jake finished up his team's part of the operation and moved to clean up. If he was quick, he realised, he could probably catch Brady for lunch.

And if that was another means of occupying his attention and avoiding Flávia, then he pretended he didn't notice.

It was only once he found himself scanning the cafeteria that he realised he was looking for Flávia.

As he always did.

Everywhere he went in this place, it seemed that he was scanning for her, listening for her, disenchanted when he didn't see her. It was foolish. Added to that, it was dangerous. This wanting...*more*.

He never wanted more. Not from any woman.

He wouldn't have categorised himself as a playboy by any standards, but he never went in for long-term relationships. When did he ever have time? Even before, when he'd been a so-called carefree bachelor. And certainly not now that he had to be responsible for his nephew.

Yet he searched for Flávia, all the same. Like he wanted their one night together to be something that it wasn't.

It was insane.

He'd even tried telling himself that the unexpected intensity of the attraction was because, since he'd become sole guardian to Brady, he hadn't had any women in his personal life, at all. The poor kid had been through enough turmoil without having his uncle bringing random women home.

Yet the other night, he'd gone and booked a suite just so he could take Flávia, a virtual stranger, to bed.

As if he hadn't been able to help himself.

He gripped his cup, willing the memories away. This attraction had to stop now. For Brady's sake, if nothing else.

As if to consolidate the idea, his nephew chose that very moment to walk through the cafeteria doors, but there were too many people milling around and Brady didn't see him. Jake stood, ready to wave, but then he saw his nephew stop dead, his attention clearly arrested by someone or something.

Standing resolutely, Jake picked up his coffee cup and strode across to the tray corral. He could still just about see Brady but now, to his surprise, the characteristically serious, silent nephew was chatting—somewhat animatedly. Jake watched, but it was next to impossible to spot people from this distance. Even so, his stomach dipped oddly when he caught sight of the back of a head sporting long, glossy waves just like Flávia's. He craned his neck for a better glimpse, but there were too many people and he still couldn't tell who the boy was talking to.

He was seeing ghosts, he reprimanded himself sharply. He'd been thinking about Flávia and so his imagination had conjured her up.

But he was here for Brady. Not her.

He would not just stay here, hoping that this woman would walk through the door any moment. He would attend her lecture, like every other doctor there using the summer programme as a chance to broaden their knowledge base and keep up to date. But other than that, he wasn't interested in seeing Flávia Maura again.

Then, tossing his rubbish into the bins, Jake weaved his way through the tables.

Flávia had been scanning through her lecture notes in the cafeteria when the young voice had penetrated her concentration.

'Did you know that the terms *venom*, *poison* and *toxin* aren't synonyms?'

She had looked up slowly, taking in a young kid with an English accent who was wearing cargo pants and *A Bug's Life* tee, which probably explained his opening question. She had followed his gaze as it flickered onto her laptop case, the VenomSci logo emblazoned on the pristine black material, then she'd glanced back at him.

Even in that moment, her traitorous heart had begun to pound a little faster. Surely, there was no one else this kid could be but Jake's nephew? Which meant Jake couldn't be far behind. She had tried in vain to stop her eyes from darting around the room, bouncing off every wall and every person, as they looked for Jake.

She'd ignored the dip of her stomach when they finally confirmed what some intuitive part of her already knew—that he wasn't there. He couldn't be. Still, the hairs on her neck had stood up with some kind of awareness.

Time to calm down, she had remonstrated herself. *Seeing Jake's nephew here was pure coincidence, nothing more.*

Except that she'd known that was a lie. There was only one reason that she had frequented Paula's Café more times in the last week than she had probably used it in the last twelve months, and that reason was about six foot two, with dark hair, and almost as serious and earnest as the boy standing at her table.

However, it was the haunted expression which had poked its way into her, scraping at her. The brief story that Jake had told her about the boy's mother had echoed painfully around her chest. Oesophageal cancer. So sudden and unpredictable. How easily could that be Julianna or Marcie?

Deus, it didn't bear thinking about.

'As it happens, I do know the difference between poison and venom,' she had acknowledged gently. 'But why don't you tell me what you think?'

The boy—Brady, if she remembered Jake rightly—had dipped his head in acknowledgement, maintaining direct eye contact but without a hint of a smile. All business.

'Both poison and venom are toxins, but it's the method of delivery that changes. Venom is injected whilst poison is secreted.'

He had delivered the facts quite animatedly, with such an intensity in his gaze that it had been like looking into a mirror to the past. For a moment, it had taken her quite aback.

Now, tugged back into the present, something slammed inside Flávia's chest. How much of her own childhood had she spent lost in knowledge, and facts, and learning, in a way that her peers simply hadn't understood? Greedily soaking up information and devouring books about anything and everything, but especially the natural world?

It had made for a rather lonely childhood, craving someone who would share her knowledge and her passion, but more often than not being thought of as a bit nerdy. Or, more likely, plain *weird.* Not least by her younger, social-butter-fly sister, who had loved her but never understood how Flávia could have preferred ants over boys. Then again, if it hadn't been for Maria dragging her to every party and social event going, maybe she would have turned out a lot more… introverted than she actually felt. At least now, in social situations, she could fool people around into thinking she was more confident than was actually the case.

Something twisted in her chest, but she pushed it aside. She wasn't that weird kid any more. She'd come out the other side a long time ago and now her life was everything she could ever have dreamed it would be. An internationally respected, cutting-edge research scientist by day, and a loved and admired best aunt in the world to her two gloriously fun nieces by evening. The perfect life. But this poor kid still wouldn't be there for about another ten years or more.

If that was, indeed, his path. Folding her hands in her lap, she cocked her head to one side. How like the seven-year-old Flávia was this boy? Did he get adults dismissing him the same way that she used to? Would he respond to someone who treated him as more than just a kid, and could talk to him on his level?

'Nice. So, do you want to give me some examples?'

A sense of victory punched through her as she saw that closed expression relax a fraction. Then he edged closer to her.

'Bees, scorpions, spiders, ants, snakes—they all deliver toxins through their bite or sting, so that's *venom*. Rough-skinned newts, poison dart frogs, cane toads—all secrete, so they're poison-ous. That's also why we say food *poisoning*, not food *venoming*.'

'I'm impressed.' She smiled widely. 'Okay, here's a bigger test. What about the Asian tiger snake?'

He narrowed his eyes.

'That's not a bigger test. It's venomous, like I said. Snakes inject through their bite.'

'Actually, as well as fangs to deliver venom, the Asian tiger snake has defensive glands on the back of its neck which deliver poison that it stores from eating poison toads, making it the only snake which is poisonous as well as ven-omous.'

It was a gamble, Flávia knew that. She wasn't intending to trap him or belittle him, although she knew other kids might have felt that way. But this kid was different, and she suspected that as long as she was feeding him more information, he wouldn't care about being wrong. He'd just store the knowledge for the future.

Still, she didn't realise she'd been holding her

breath until the boy's eyes widened and he edged forward again.

'What else do you know that I don't?' he demanded, almost breathless with excitement.

'I'm willing to bet lots.' Flávia grinned, relieved when he smiled back. 'But first, how about we find who you're here with?'

She couldn't bring herself to say Jake, but when he backed up almost imperceptibly, and his little face shuttered down, she could have kicked herself for not thinking faster.

'My mummy died last year.'

'I'm sorry, Brady. It is Brady, isn't it?'

He nodded.

'I know you're here with your uncle. I just meant, who is looking after you now? A hospital nurse?'

'Patricia,' he confirmed after a moment, jerking to an older woman paying for something at the counter. 'She's getting me a meal. Then Uncle Jake will meet me here.'

'Soon?'

'Whenever he finishes.' He shrugged, that sadness swirling around him again.

He might as well have slammed her in the chest. Flávia fought to breathe. It was all she could do to stay composed.

'I see,' she managed.

The silence moved around them, and then

Brady narrowed his eyes—eyes which must have been identical to his mother's given how closely they resembled Jake's blue depths.

'Why do you work for a company called VenomSci? Do you use animal venom? Do you hurt them?'

It was the distraction she needed.

'Quite the opposite,' she assured him. 'I've worked with wasp venom, scorpion venom and snake venom. But whatever project I work on for pharmaceutical companies, my personal goal remains the same, and that's finding ways to protect and save as many animals as possible.'

He eyed her suspiciously.

'Why would I believe you?'

'I don't know. But I have a nine-year-old niece and a six-year-old niece, and we often go exploring the forest together to see what we can find, and which animals we can help.'

Although she never let the girls go near anything that could possibly harm them.

He scrutinised her for a little longer.

'Promise?'

'I promise.'

They eyed each other for a few moments, and she knew he was assessing her. Evaluating. Just the way that she would have done at that age.

'Brady? *Brady?* Why aren't you with Patricia? What are you doing here?'

It was the moment she told herself she'd been dreading. It took everything she had not to spin around in her chair, but instead she waited for him to draw level with her table.

'Jake.' She inclined her head as professionally as she could. 'I already checked where Patricia was, and she's right over there by the counter.'

'I was coming to sit down when we…' Brady paused, looking to her.

'Flávia,' she supplied helpfully.

'Flávia and I started taking about venom and poison.'

'Is that so?' Jake bit out, eyeing her as if she had somehow engineered the situation.

Evidently, he'd had no intention of seeking her out after their night together, and probably would have been more than happy if their paths hadn't crossed for the remainder of his stay in Brazil.

She told herself she didn't care, that she'd known the parameters of their…*encounter* the night of the party. But the way her throat was closing, and the shameful stinging behind her eyes, told her a different story.

Idiot that she was.

'How did you get talking, anyway?'

'Because she knows about nature, too.' The kid looked at his uncle as though the answer was surely obvious.

Clearly, Jake wasn't convinced.

'He spotted my laptop case.' She gestured to the bright logo. 'It caught his interest.'

'Ah…' Jake surveyed the case, and if he didn't actually roll his eyes, then he at least gave the impression of dismissal. 'That would have done it. He's obsessed with everything from ants to cheetahs. How they live, how they feed, how they defend themselves.'

'Fascinated,' Flávia corrected automatically, unable to help herself.

'Sorry?'

'He's *fascinated*. Not *obsessed*. There's a difference.'

It was like a mini stand-off, but Flávia couldn't bring herself to regret it. She told herself she was just looking out for the child. She suspected a part of her was also trying to help Jake make that connection he hadn't been able to bring himself to outright admit to her was lacking.

'The difference is called *hyperfocus*,' he told her, his tone clipped.

She glanced at Brady, and this time it was her turn to do a little assessing. He stared right back at her with intelligent—if sad—eyes, a slightly cheeky set to his mouth and a vaguely mutinous look to his stance.

She didn't see *hyperfocus*, or any other issue that she imagined people might have thrown at Jake over the past ten months. She just saw a bright little boy, grieving for his mother, possibly too bright for his own good, probably considered cheeky or disruptive in school and misunderstood by the adults around him.

She saw herself.

But where she'd had her father, always there to encourage her curiosity and teach her new experiences, she wasn't sure Brady had the same level of support. Though, it was clear that he had an uncle trying desperately to do his best.

She could shut her mouth and stay out of it, or she could try helping both Brady and Jake, all the while knowing that she risked Jake believing she was using his nephew to wedge herself into their lives after what had been, for all intents and purposes, a one-night stand.

Finally, decision made, she turned back to Jake.

'Maybe,' she answered coolly, even though her heart was now threatening to beat right out of her chest. Though not necessarily for the same reasons as before. 'But I don't think so.'

He could see the fury in Jake, in the tight set of his jaw, and the tiny pulse flickering in his neck, though he reined it in admirably.

'Brady,' he addressed his nephew in an eerily calm voice. 'Please join Patricia for a moment.'

'But I wanted to ask Flávia some more questions.' The boy frowned, apparently oblivious to Jake's anger.

'*Now*, Brady,' Jake instructed. 'Please.'

He waited until his nephew was an adequate distance away before he turned his gaze back to her. The fury in his gaze almost blistering her skin everywhere it fell, though regrettably not for the same reasons as the other night.

'Listen—'

'Not here,' he cut her off harshly, leaving her no choice but to grab her bag and stand.

No sooner had he done so than he took hold of her elbow—not roughly, but not with the tenderness of the other night, either—and ushered her out of the room, down a corridor and into the first unoccupied room he could.

And Flávia steeled herself for the inevitable onslaught.

'What the hell do you think you're playing at?'

CHAPTER SIX

HE COULD SEE the flinty look in Flávia's eyes as he challenged her. A part of him even admired her for it.

But not when she was pulling Brady into some game.

Rage coursed through him…and something else. Something it took him a while to recognise.

Disappointment, he realised darkly. He was disappointed in Flávia.

He couldn't explain why, since one night of sex hardly equated to a deep knowledge of another person, but that simply wasn't the way he would ever have expected Flávia to behave.

'I'm not playing at anything, Jake.' Her honey-hued eyes gleamed. 'I'm trying to look out for a little boy.'

'You believe that I'm *not*?' he barked.

'I don't believe I commented on you, whatsoever,' she answered evenly, though he could see the hectic racing of her pulse at her neck.

'You don't know the first thing about Brady, and yet you feel you have the right to judge him. Why? Because we slept together once? I have news for you, Flávia—I have had a fair few one-night stands in my life, and they tried many things to draw more of a relationship out of it, but none of them acted so low as to bring a seven-year-old boy into it.'

He'd intended to throw the verbal punch, but when it hit home, when she recoiled, he felt… *remorse. Regret.*

Then, to his surprise, she straightened herself and faced him boldly.

'I dare say that's because you only took responsibility for Brady ten months ago. If he'd been around when those kinds of women had tried to ingratiate themselves into your life, then I imagine some of them might have thought he was fair game.'

He inhaled sharply but then, astonishingly, she held her hand up to silence him.

'I, however, do not think he's *fair game*. But for what it's worth, I know more about boys like Brady than you might think.'

'Is that so?'

'There's something special about Brady.' She smiled, a soft smile which inexplicably made Jake feel as though he was intruding on her personal memories. 'And I'm willing to bet that it doesn't fit with whatever you've been told about him being a difficult kid in school. I think you know it, too.'

Jake faltered. Her words made more sense than

he'd have liked to admit. Before he could answer, she had started talking again.

'And, for the record, I have no interest in drawing out *anything* with you.'

She was lying. He knew it as surely as he knew his own name. He knew it in the way her pupils dilated when she looked at him, the way her pulse still raced and the way her cheeks flushed slightly.

And he knew it in the way his entire body reacted to her.

One night hadn't sated the extraordinary attraction between them. If anything, it had only made their chemistry stronger.

It was baffling. Yet here he was, drawn in, compelled to hear whatever else Flávia had to say. Though, whether it was for Brady's sake, or simply his own selfish desire to prolong any contact with her, Jake couldn't be sure.

'What do you think you know about kids like Brady?' He gritted his teeth. 'Or is it just because he happens to have this damned obsession with venom, or snakes, or whatever?'

She actually snorted at him—even if he heard a faint shake behind the sound.

'Sorry—a *fascination*,' he corrected, remembering her earlier words. 'As if it makes that much difference.'

She sucked in a breath, composing herself.

'It does make a difference,' she insisted. 'Listen, I can see that you care for your nephew, and that you're trying to do your best in a really horrible situation. But labels matter. Attitudes matter. And how you help Brady matters.'

'I appreciate your attempt to help…' He really wanted to say something else, but decided it wasn't the best idea. Her words echoed Oz's only too closely, if a little more forthrightly, and it hit him again how little he knew about kids—any kids—but especially about his little nephew. 'But you really don't know what you're talking about.'

'I *know*.' She scowled.

'How?' he pressed, uncertain why it mattered. Was he asking for Brady? Or was there a part of him that was hungry to know Flávia better? 'How do you know?'

'It isn't relevant.'

He could feel his patience fraying and snagging at the edges. He just wasn't sure why.

'When you're standing here telling me I'm not doing the best thing for my nephew, and that you believe the things I've been told are wrong, believe me, it matters. So, I'll ask you one more time, Flávia—how do you know?'

She glared at him, her teeth bared in something of a snarl, and he got the sense that she wanted something said without actually wanting to utter the words.

Just when he thought she was going to concede the argument, or discussion, or whatever it was that they were even having, she squared up to him and spoke.

'Because I *was* a Brady.'

The words hung there, between them, shimmering like a curtain.

'What do you mean, *you were a Brady*? What is *a Brady*? He's just a normal kid retreating into a subject that he's decided has caught his interest, because his mother is dead.'

He nearly choked on the words. Nearly choked on the guilt that had followed him around like a dark cloud ever since he'd failed to save his sister's life.

'I don't think so.' She shook her head.

'Then what?'

'I don't think it's *hyperfocus*, ADD, ADHD or whatever else schoolteachers, doctors, other professionals may have told you—and don't get me wrong, I know those conditions are very real for some kids, but not for Brady.'

'So what, in your professional opinion, is it?'

He heard the edge of sarcasm in his tone, just as he heard the edge of desperation and hope.

'It's nothing.' She shrugged. 'At least, not like you're thinking. But you don't have to take my word for it. How about when you have a free moment today, maybe between operations, you bring him to VenomSci's visitor centre and we'll find out?'

'Music, please,' Jake requested, making the first incision as the first song on his playlist filled the operating room.

At least with this, his first teaching operation instead of just lecture room talks and video presentations, he finally had something to really get his teeth into, and switch his head off from Silvio Delgado's most recent shenanigans.

And from more run-ins with Flávia.

Why the heck had he gone at her so hard in the cafeteria? He could pretend it had been about protecting Brady, but he knew that wasn't it.

No, he'd been making a point of proving to her—and, more pertinently, himself—that their night together had been a one-off. That he harboured no lingering desires.

He knew it was a lie. Still, he wasn't certain how taking Brady to VenomSci's visitor centre was designed to help, but there was a part of him which welcomed the opportunity just to change the dialogue between them.

'I realise you've been thrown in at the deep end on this case and haven't had a chance to do surgical rounds on the patients in my clinical trial.'

He glanced up at the new surgical intern, after a while. 'But it will be a great learning opportunity for you. So talk me through what you *do* know about this patient.'

It wasn't the intern's fault that Delgado had stirred things up by claiming the intern, who had been shadowing Jake for the past week, for a surgery of his own this afternoon. Typical Delgado, still smarting from Jake's perceived snub at the Welcome Gala, and trying to stamp his authority all over the hospital.

'The patient is a thirty-five-year-old female. She has *dermatofibrosarcoma protuberans*—a rare type of soft-tissue sarcoma developing in the deep layers of the skin.'

'So how would you normally expect to operate on the patient?' Jake asked, his eyes on the patient and the image on the monitors.

'Resect the tumour by cutting a two-centre margin around the sarcoma. If they come back negative, then you've cleared the tumour and there's a very low chance that the cancer should return.'

'Good,' Jake confirmed, continuing his work until he was satisfied. 'Now what we're actually going to do is this…lights, please.'

As the OR went dark, the familiar glow could be seen on the patient's body. As Jake had anticipated, the dye showed the sarcoma to clearly be larger than images had been able to identify, reaching out in multiple directions and travelling from the dermis, quite deeply down.

'So there it is.'

The intern peered in.

'It's like our own personal markers,' he breathed.

'Right. No guesswork needed. No taking healthy tissue unnecessarily as part of the margins. But more significantly, no inadvertently leaving behind unidentified tumour, thinking that we've actually got it all. DFSP is one of those sarcomas where local recurrence is particularly common if the resection is incomplete.'

'So no intraoperative freezing to cut sections for biopsy?'

'We'll still do that as we resect the tumour, then we'll close with a skin graft, and follow up with vacuum sealing negative pressure drainage.'

Flávia watched Jake usher Brady through the doors of the centre and told herself that she didn't really feel her pulse hammering through her veins like air in the old radiator system of her first city apartment.

Especially pretending that she didn't feel it pulsing at her neck, her nipples, her core.

Part of her hadn't really thought he'd come, though she'd wanted him to.

For the kid's sake, she reminded herself hastily.

But she plastered a smile on her face and crossed the room.

'Jake, Brady, I'm so glad you came. This way, please.'

'What is it you want to prove?' Jake muttered as they followed her through the centre and to the area she wanted them to see.

But Flávia was already paying attention to Brady, at the way his eyes widened, beamed and then focused as he glanced around the space. A Ferris wheel spun slowly, with a projection behind, showing different rainforest animals and their habitats and prey. There was an interactive area with knowledge-based quizzes, games showing mimicry in nature and challenging the player to tell one from the other and an arcade-style machine for the life cycle of a butterfly.

And Brady was utterly fascinated.

'What exactly is the point of this?' Jake demanded after ten minutes or so.

'Give it time and you'll find out,' she instructed him. 'Now, go to the gallery over there, get a coffee, sit down and just watch.'

She could feel his eyes boring into her as she deliberately turned her back on him, and the barely suppressed fury. Yet he obeyed. Clearly, despite the way he had presented the facts in the past, his nephew meant more to him than just a responsibility his sister had left on him.

Flávia filed that away for later.

Then, she watched as Brady made his way into the interactive area, taking in each game and experiment and weighing each of them up as he decided which one to look at first. Evidently torn.

'This one is all about mimicry in nature.' She tried to help him, selecting one of the games and taking a few steps towards it, to see if Brady followed her. 'Do you recognise any of them?'

He practically skipped behind her.

'That pair is a viceroy butterfly and a monarch butterfly—the viceroy mimics the monarch, which tastes horrible to predators because of its milkweed diet as a caterpillar. That pair is a bushveld lizard and an oogpister beetle, and the beetle tastes horrible to predators because of the formic acid due to its diet of army ants. And that pair is a wasp spider and a wasp, which it kind of self-explanatory.'

'Good.' Flávia nodded. 'Although the viceroy and monarch butterflies are now thought to show mutual mimicry, as the viceroy can release its own toxins when stressed, which makes it equally unpalatable to predators.'

'Really?' Brady stared at her in wonder.

'Sure. Look, if you press that button you can start the game and learn more.'

The boy didn't need any more encouragement, and Flávia backed off to let him have his head.

For over an hour she accompanied him around the room, letting him choose what to try next, only giving guidance to information when Brady invited it. Nonetheless, it was a good hour later before he finally showed signs of becoming saturated, and she called him for a short break, watching as he enjoyed his slushie, his eyes still roaming the room, from the activities he'd enjoyed the most to those he evidently still wanted to try.

And then, unexpectedly, he turned his serious eyes on her.

'Are you Uncle Jake's girlfriend?'

'I...no.' Flávia fought against getting flustered. 'I'm just a colleague.'

'Oh.'

There was no mistaking the disappointment in his tone, and despite everything in her screaming to leave it alone, Flávia couldn't help herself.

'Does your uncle have lots of girlfriends, then?'

'No.' Brady took another sip of his drink. 'Mummy told me that he might do, before she died. But he hasn't. Not until you.'

He was so calm, so collected, but Flávia hadn't missed the way he'd steeled himself before he'd spoken. Jake had told her that Brady didn't seem to want to grieve at all for his mother, but she suspected that wasn't right.

'You must miss your mummy a lot.'

The little boy stopped drinking. He stared at his glass.

'I miss her all the time.'

'Do you talk about her, with your uncle?' she asked quietly, even though she already knew what Jake had told her.

'No.'

'Why not?' she pressed gently.

'I think it makes him sad.' He sucked in a breath. 'It makes me sad, too, sometimes. But it also makes me happy to remember her. I don't think it makes Uncle Jake happy to remember Mummy. I think he would prefer to forget her.'

Her heart almost broke for the little boy. Brady *did* grieve for his mother. He just held it in, keeping it away from Jake because he didn't want to hurt his uncle. The way she had done with her father when her mother had walked out on the family.

Only, she'd been lucky. She'd had her sister to talk to.

'Oh, Brady, I don't think that's true. I think your uncle would hate to know you felt you couldn't talk about your mummy to him. I don't think he'd want you to forget her.'

'I won't forget her. I have a memory box. Mummy and I made it together when I was a kid.'

'Does it have photos?'

She didn't like to point out that, at seven years old, he still was a kid.

'Lots and lots of photos.' He nodded. 'And flowers we picked on picnics, the programme for a football game we went to, cinema tickets, museum tickets, tickets to our favourite film…' He trailed off. 'It's in England, though. So I can't show you.'

'And you've never shown your uncle?'

'No, but I nearly showed Oz once.'

'Who's Oz?'

'He's Uncle Jake's best friend. He's kinda cool and he *does* have a lot of girlfriends. I talk to him about Mummy sometimes, but not always. I don't want Uncle Jake to hear and be upset.'

'What about you? Do you have a best friend? In school, maybe?'

'Not really.' He shook his head. 'I did have one at my old school, but I had to leave it because Uncle Jake works in London, and they're not as friendly in my new school. Sometimes they crawl under the table when the teacher is out of the room and slap my legs. And they play games I don't know, or won't let me join in because in my old school we had different rules. I bet you had a lot of best friends when you were in school.'

'I'll let you into a little secret,' Flávia whispered, wishing with every fibre of her being that she could haul the little boy into her arms and cuddle all his unhappiness away. But she couldn't bring back his mum, and that was the one thing he would really want. 'I didn't have many friends in school, either.'

'So, what did you do?'

'I was lucky. I had my sister,' she admitted. 'And when I came home I had *papai* and *vovô*. My dad and my granddad.'

'I have a granddad. And a grandma. But I only met them once. Mummy didn't like them. She said that they weren't unkind but that they were very cold, and they didn't know how to show love. She told me that was why she wanted me to live with Uncle Jake.'

'Because he knew how to show love?' Flávia managed, her heart breaking all over again.

'She said he could learn, but my granddad and grandma never could. She said Uncle Jake was a good brother when they were little, they had just gone different ways when they grew older. She told me it was going to be my job to teach him how to love. Because she thought he could, he just doesn't know how to. But I don't know how to teach him.' He looked up at her abruptly, his eyes swimming. 'He isn't like Mummy and I don't know what I'm supposed to do.'

She glanced up to where Jake was in the gallery, but he wasn't there. Hoping against hope he was on his way down, Flávia didn't think twice.

She moved around the table, her arms going around the tiny, shaking body, her mouth pressed to his head, her voice low and soothing. And if it was a little choked up, she prayed that Brady couldn't tell.

'You're not supposed to do anything, sweetheart. You're doing everything right, trust me. I know your uncle loves you, very much. I just don't think he knows how to show it, but I think you can teach him. Just like your mummy believed you could.'

'You have to help me,' he whispered fiercely.

She wasn't sure that she was the best person to teach anybody about love. Sure, she loved her family with everything she had, but she didn't know how to love anybody else. Hadn't Enrico taught her that much? Hadn't he pointed out how selfish she was when he called off their engagement? How wrong she was for being unwilling to sacrifice the dangers of her career for a life with him?

He'd made her choose between risking her life with her deadly snakes, and marrying him and having a family. And she'd wished she could choose him. She'd wished she could be the kind of person who would *want* to choose love.

But she'd had to accept the fact that she wasn't that kind of person. When it had come down to it, she'd been afraid that she would end up resenting him for making the ultimatum and so, in the end, she'd chosen her snakes.

So how was she the right kind of person to help Brady teach Jake *anything* about self-sacrificing love?

Besides, there was no question that Jake would hate her inserting herself into their lives. Into *his* life.

But how could she refuse when Brady was asking so desperately? When he was clinging to her as though she was his life raft in his own personal storm? When she could feel his wet tears soaking into her cotton tee?

'It's okay, sweetheart. I'll help you as much as I can.'

CHAPTER SEVEN

JAKE HAMMERED THE punchbag, over and over and over again. Anything to get rid of this suffocating emotion which had come over him in that visitor centre when he'd watched Flávia with his nephew. When he'd heard Brady taking to her, spilling his heart to her, connecting with her, in a way Brady hadn't done, even once, in their ten months together.

He'd left the gallery partway through Brady's confession, intent on coming in and setting the record straight. Telling his nephew that he would never have avoided conversation about Helen if he'd realised that Brady wanted to talk about his mother.

But as he'd stood in the doorway and watched Flávia cradle the little boy in her arms, he had frozen. A thousand self-recriminations chasing through his head.

What the hell did he even say to the boy?

The simple fact was that he should have *known* that Brady would want—*need*—to talk about his mother. He hadn't avoided the topic purely out of respect for Brady's space—the kid was only seven. *No*, he'd used that as an excuse to help *himself* avoid conversation which might include things as complicated, as *icky*, as feelings.

Helen had been right in that their own parents hadn't prepared them for or taught them about love. But she had been wrong thinking that he had the capacity to learn it now.

So what use was he to Brady?

He, who had never failed at anything in his life before?

And so, he'd stood there at the door, watching a relative stranger give his nephew the kind of love and comfort he himself had no idea how to show. He'd tried to force his legs to move, to carry him inside, to say any one of the caring things that tripped easily off his tongue when dealing with frightened cancer patients and their even more terrified families. But his body and brain had refused to work. He'd been immobile. Numb. Until suddenly, he'd found himself moving again. Only, he hadn't been heading into the room with his nephew; instead, he'd been halfway across the hospital grounds, calling Patricia to let her know where to collect Brady for their usual afternoon session, whilst he'd thrown himself into his next operation.

Ironic how residents and colleagues thanked him for his quiet, efficient teaching style, whilst the one person he couldn't teach, or even talk to, was a seven-year-old kid who needed him most.

And so, after the operation, he'd wound up here, in the gym complex within the hospital guest accommodations. People were out there in the main area, on treadmills, or rowing machines, or whatever, but in this small side room, with the boxing equipment, he felt as though he was in his own little world. He could belt seven shades out of a punchbag and hope to hell he could simultaneously beat some sense into himself.

He kept seeing Flávia's face, hearing her words, but it wasn't her whom he was mad with. It was himself. And his own inabilities.

Of all the people with whom to have left her infinitely precious son, Helen had chosen him. Not for the first time, Jake seriously doubted the rationale of his sister's decision.

Who would ever have considered him, so famously detached for all his life, to take up the role of a surrogate father?

Surely, even his parents—Brady's grandparents—would have been a better choice?

In spite of everything.

Jake slammed his gloved fists into the bag again.

He was going to mess it all up. Mess Brady up. He didn't have a clue how to care for the boy properly; today had taught him that much. He'd been too quick to accept all the explanations that people had given him. Whether it was to blame

Brady's wild actions on the fact that his mother had died ten months ago, or to blame his refusal to communicate with others on a genuine physical and mental inability to do so.

Flávia had come along, and in one afternoon she'd turned all of that on its head.

She'd shown him a bright, engaged and engaging seven-year-old. A *normal* kid who was obviously grieving over the death of his mother, but who wasn't irreparably damaged.

She had seen all that. And he'd seen nothing. So he had to ask himself if that would still be the case in another year—in six months, even—of Brady being in his care.

Again and again, he slammed his fists into the bag. But none of it did any good. None of it changed anything. Until, suddenly something lifted. And he knew, in that instant, that he was no longer alone. Flávia had walked into the gym.

Jake stopped. Not turning around. Just waiting.

'So this is where you went.'

She didn't even bother to disguise the accusation in her voice and he didn't blame her. Even as he lied.

'I had a teaching operation to get to,' he said over his shoulder, still not turning.

'You heard our conversation, didn't you.' It was phrased as a question but it was more of a statement. 'From the gallery.'

He exhaled deeply.

'I heard most of it.'

'You heard him say that he never talked about his mother because he was upset that it hurt you too much.'

The admission had walloped into him hard enough when he'd heard it come out of his nephew's mouth. Coming out of Flávia's mouth, it lacerated just as much.

'I heard,' he managed thickly.

'And?'

'*And?*' he managed incredulously, finally turning around.

'Yes.' She gazed at him evenly. 'And…?'

'How do you think it feels?' he growled.

'Why don't you try telling me?'

All of a sudden he realised what she was doing. He snorted. Loudly.

'You really think me telling you how guilty, how bad, I feel will suddenly put me in touch with feelings we both know I don't have?'

'Don't you think it might be a start?' she challenged. And suddenly, he couldn't argue with her.

Or maybe you don't want *to argue with her?*

'Fine,' he shot at her. 'I feel like crap. I just had to listen to my seven-year-old nephew say that he has been hiding a box of memories of his mummy because he was trying to protect me.

When *I'm* the one who is supposed to be protecting *him*.'

'So talk to him about it.'

'You don't think I've tried? I can't—I think that much should be obvious to you by now.'

'Didn't your parents teach you never to believe in that word *can't*?'

'My parents didn't teach me much at all. They expected the private school Helen and I attended to do that. But sure, I never believed in that word up to ten months ago, only now I do. If you hadn't been there today, I still wouldn't know any of those things he said. So, I can't talk to Brady. I don't know how to.'

'Then learn,' she bit out. 'You're bright—heck, you're a top oncologist. You can learn if you want to, and that little boy needs you to learn. He needs you to take care of him.'

'And I will. Materially, anyway.'

She snorted, throwing her hands up in the air.

'He needs more than that. He needs your love, Jake.'

'And I can't do that. Helen knew that, but she entrusted Brady to me, anyway.'

'She also believed in you enough to think that you could learn.'

'She was wrong.'

'Is this because of your parents? Is what Brady said about them true?'

He didn't want to answer her—it wasn't any of her business. But the closer Flávia got, the more she pushed, the less wound up he seemed to feel. She had an uncanny knack of highlighting his shortcomings, yet simultaneously make him feel as though she could help solve them.

It made no sense.

'They did their duty by us. Neither Helen nor I were ever hurt or mistreated by them.'

'That's basically what Brady said. But it doesn't fully answer the question, does it?'

'It isn't relevant,' he deflected.

'We both know that it is. Unless you're happy with your relationship with your nephew, that is. And we both know that you aren't.'

'Well, talking about it isn't going to change that, is it?'

Jake didn't know what he expected her to say, but it wasn't what she came out with.

'You're right. I can't *tell* you how to treat Brady, how to connect with him. But maybe I can show you.'

'Show me?' he echoed sceptically.

'He loves animals, and the natural world. Why not let me take you both into the rainforest for a day or two? Doing something new like that, something he loves but with which he has no residual memories of his mother, might help the two of you connect. Build some memories of your own.'

'I don't think so.' The refusal was out before he'd even engaged his brain.

'Why not? Brady would love it!'

Jake opened his mouth to reply, but couldn't bring himself to tell her that he'd heard the rumours about the way she risked her life. He didn't want to say that he was worried she would risk Brady's.

He found he didn't want to hurt her.

So what did that say?

'I'm not exactly an authority on the rainforest. I wouldn't know how to keep myself safe, so how can I keep a seven-year-old safe?'

She wrinkled her nose and, without warning, looked awkward, and he would have given anything to know what she was thinking in that instant.

'Then why not try smaller?' she suggested after a moment.

'Smaller?'

'My sister is having a barbecue at the weekend. There'll be lots of people there, but especially my family. My nieces. Brady said he didn't have many friends at his new school and I wonder how much is Brady's lack of confidence. Julianna and Marcie are sweet, and funny, and friendly. They would love Brady, and you can help him to get out of himself, and start building new, positive experiences with you. It might even take some of the pressure off you so that you can find a way to let the kid in.'

'You're inviting me to a family barbecue?'

She huffed as though she was irritated, but he could see her level of discomfort grow.

'From everything I said, *that*'s the point you're hung up on?'

'I'm just trying to establish exactly what it is you're suggesting.'

'I'm trying to help your nephew,' she snapped, a little too tightly.

He should refuse. They'd had a one-night stand; he wasn't looking to make some kind of relationship out of it. And yet, the idea of going was more appealing than it ought to be.

'I'm not using Brady to try to score points with you,' she added, bristling.

'I know,' he replied, and the odd thing was that he did know.

The more worrying point was that he found he was slightly disappointed that she wasn't looking for some kind of excuse, though.

As Jake leaned against the wall, the cool of the concrete seeping through to his shoulder, and watched Brady trailing happily around the garden with Flávia's nieces, Julianna and Marcie, it wasn't all that hard to admit that Flávia had been right.

Watching Brady relax, and gain acceptance with his peers, did somehow help him to feel more relaxed. Less pressured. And all the trio were doing was wandering around the garden, their heads pressed tightly together.

Brady would listen avidly as they taught him the Portuguese names of different plants and insects, then he would teach the girls the Latin names where he knew them. Otherwise, all three children would huddle around the phone he had lent them as they looked up the missing, vital information.

Emotions tumbled through him, almost too fast to separate them, but for the first time he was beginning to think he could see a way to connect with his nephew. At long last. He sighed to himself. It was a complicated business, looking after a child. The struggles he'd had with Brady these past ten months had given him a new appreciation for all his sister had contended with, all these years as a single mother. And it augmented his sense of guilt that he should have reached out to her more over the past few years.

Was it self-deceptive to think if he had done that, Helen might still be alive today?

Possibly. But it didn't stop the thought from lurking there, in the back of his head.

'He looks happy.'

Jake turned at the sound of Maria's voice. Her voice was so similar to Flávia's, with basically identical intonations and emphases, and yet even from a distance he knew instantly who was talking in any given conversation. As though his whole being was programmed to tune into Flávia and no one else.

Already.

Which might have sounded alarm bells if he hadn't pretended to ignore it.

'Yes, he does.' Jake turned back to watch his nephew. 'Thanks again for inviting us here. I know Patricia does her best to entertain him, but it's not the same.'

With a soft smile, Maria leaned on the concrete pillar opposite his and took a sip of wine.

'I don't doubt it. And, as for the invitation, that was all Livvy,' she confessed, and he loved the affection in the nickname Maria had for her sister.

The woman paused as though thinking twice about something, then seemed to decide to say it, anyway.

'I think Brady reminds her of herself.'

Jake frowned.

'She said something like that before, but I didn't understand it.'

He didn't realise he was waiting, almost on edge, hoping for more than this unexpected scrap of information relating to Flávia, until Maria shrugged almost dismissively.

'It's hard to describe. It isn't anything I could put my finger on, just the little things. The things that make her stand out from the average person now were the things which made it hard for her to make friends in school. I suspect you know what I mean, though.'

It didn't even begin to answer all the questions he realised he had about Flávia. But he told himself that was no bad thing. He shouldn't care, anyway. That one night had been...extraordinary. To match the unique Flávia. But it had to remain a one-off. It couldn't happen again.

For Brady's sake, he wouldn't allow it.

Just for Brady? a voice needled. But Jake ignored it.

'That said,' Maria continued, 'I don't see him having any trouble with my girls.'

'No, they're getting along really well,' he acknowledged, surprised. 'I think coming here has been the best move I could have made for Brady.'

'I take it you didn't want to?' Maria asked. 'Livvy strong-armed you?'

'Maybe a little.' Although a part of him had been only too happy to let her. 'Turns out she was right, though.'

'Yeah, she has a maddening ability to do that.' The quiet laugh filled the air around them. So like Flávia's, and yet it didn't crawl inside him the way her laughter did. As though it was filling him from the inside out.

'Was she always so maddening?' he asked.

'You'd better believe it.' Maria laughed. 'The scrapes I had to get her out of when we were kids. She was so intolerant of others, saying exactly what she thought with no filter. Papai told me that it was my role to be her protector and so I did. She never thanked me for it.'

'I bet.'

He was soaking up the information with a thirst that shouldn't quite fit, but he couldn't stop himself. He wanted to know more about Flávia. As if it could somehow sate that ache inside him.

The...*yearning* he hadn't been able to quench ever since that night in his suite.

'Brady gets into fights in school,' he made himself say, as if reminding himself why he was supposed to be at Flávia's family's house in the first place. 'I thought it was a result of the trauma he has gone through with his mother's death, and having to move schools, and be in London with me. But it turns out he always had some problems, even at his old school. Nothing serious, you understand. And it isn't as though he can't make any friends.'

'He's just intolerant of so-called *idiots* in his

class?' Maria guessed. 'Those who don't want to learn and so disrupt the class?'

'To the extent where he stands up and tries to give them punishments, as though he's the teacher.'

Maria threw her head back and emitted a happy, infectious laugh.

'Yeah, that's just like Livvy.'

'She offered to take Brady into the rainforest, you know.' The words were out before Jake could second-guess himself. 'With me, of course.'

'I think Brady would really like that.'

'I know.'

'But...?' Maria prompted lightly when he didn't elaborate. 'You clearly have reservations.'

Jake stared across the garden. This was arguably dangerous ground; he risked offending Maria, and ultimately Flávia. But he had to ask. This was potentially his nephew's safety at stake.

'I've heard the stories—' he pulled a face '—that Flávia can be reckless.'

'I see.'

'I don't like rumours. But if it's true that she spent a year handling vipers even when she knew there wasn't enough antivenom on hand in the event that she got bitten, how can it be responsible of me to let her take us into that kind of environment?'

He didn't realise how badly he'd wanted to hear Maria laugh and declare it to be absolute rubbish until she stayed silent, the air thickening around them with every passing moment.

Suddenly, his shoulder felt like a block of ice, frozen tightly to the cold, concrete pillar. He, who was rarely wrong about anything in his life, had never wished he could be more wrong than he did in this instant.

'So it's also true that she ended up getting bitten?'

The silence seemed to grow heavier somehow. And louder. Or perhaps that was just his own blood, thundering through his veins.

And then, at last, Maria spoke.

'You really should speak to Livvy about that.'

Silence weaved around him for a moment. Then he offered a tight nod.

'I'm the closest thing Brady has to a father right now. And you have two kids of your own. So I'm asking you.'

Another beat. Then Maria scrunched up her face.

'I can tell you this,' she told him firmly. 'My sister is passionate, and focused, and driven. And maybe she does take occasional risks when it comes to her own life out there. But she has never, *ever* taken a risk with someone else's life.'

'I don't know that it helps,' Jake began, finding he had to fight to try to get his head around Maria's words.

'Then maybe this will. I know what Livvy does can be dangerous. A matter of life and death, even. And sometimes I do look out at the jungle when I know she's in there, wondering if she's going to come back safely. But I've never once felt that way when she's been out there with one of my girls.'

'She takes Julianna and Marcie?'

'She does,' Maria declared. 'She and Papai have taken the girls out there at least twice this past year. And on those occasions, I never looked out over that rainforest and wondered if they were okay. Because I knew that she would take care of my daughters in a way she never thinks to take care of herself.'

'I see.' He nodded slowly. 'I just didn't think of it that way. Flávia told me that she was *the fun aunt*. I guess I assumed that also meant...'

'That she wasn't entirely responsible with them?'

He eyed her sharply but there was no judgement in Maria's expression.

'I suppose.'

'I understand why,' she continued. 'But no, that isn't what Livvy is like at all. That's what Enrico couldn't seem to get his head around.'

'Enrico?'

'Her ex-fiancé.' Maria rolled her eyes. 'Idiot man.'

It was irrational. And insane. But jealousy swept through him like a tsunami, and even though he tried to pull himself up, it was too late. He'd waded in too deep and now he couldn't get out.

'Who's an idiot man?'

They both swung around at the sound of Flávia's voice.

'Boy, do you both look guilty.' She tried for a laugh when they didn't answer. 'Never mind. You don't have to tell me.'

'I wasn't going to.' Maria laughed at last as she turned around to leave, dropping a kiss on her sister's cheek as she did so. 'I think I'll leave you to it while I go and find my husband.'

'Luis has his chef's cap on. He looks set for the night.'

'Great. That means I can grab another wine and find somewhere else to hide before he drags me in to help him.'

'Yeah, good luck with that,' joked Flávia, watching her sister go.

Just as Jake, in turn, was watching Flávia.

As though he had no choice in it. Because he seemed to have very little control over himself when it came to Flávia Maura.

And then they were alone, and he found himself fighting some inexplicably primal urge to grab and kiss her, and make her his—over and over—when she started to speak.

CHAPTER EIGHT

'WHY WERE YOU talking about Enrico?' she asked carefully.

'You heard that, huh?'

If she'd hoped to decipher anything from his tone, then she realised she was out of luck. She had to force herself to keep her own voice deliberately even.

'I heard Maria tell you he was my ex-fiancé.'

'Was it recent?'

Was he asking out of simple curiosity? Or something more?

'We broke up two years ago.' She shrugged. 'Dated for eight years before that.'

He cocked one eyebrow.

'And since then…?'

'There's been no one but you,' she confirmed, her eyes locked with his, almost daring him to comment.

But he didn't.

'How did it end?'

She scowled at him like it was none of his business. Yet she answered him, anyway. It was like a compulsion. He'd asked and she had to answer.

Though she'd never talked about Enrico to anyone but her family.

Then again, she'd been experiencing a plethora of firsts ever since Jake had approached her at that Welcome Gala.

'He gave me an ultimatum. Him or the sanctuary.'

'You chose your snakes,' he guessed.

'I shouldn't have had to choose.' She frowned, willing him to understand. As though his opinion mattered to her. 'There was no need.'

'He cared about you. He didn't want you to get bitten again. I can see where your ex was coming from.'

He sounded almost...*angry* about it. But that didn't make sense.

'I've been bitten plenty of times over the years.' She narrowed her eyes. 'It's a hazard of my career.'

'Maybe, but have you always risked a bite when there's been no antivenom on hand?'

She watched him in silence, not sure why he sounded so accusatory.

'It happened years ago,' she spoke at last.

'Sorry?'

'The incident people talk about. It happened years ago,' she repeated, as coolly and calmly as she could. 'There *were* actually some vials of antivenom, though admittedly not enough.

'The government had received a complaint from some high-ranking official whose condo backed onto the sanctuary's land.' She leaned sideways and flopped her shoulder against the concrete pillar opposite his. 'I believe the guy wanted to build an extension, but he couldn't build that close to his boundary so he decided the solution was to acquire sanctuary land. But the sanctuary is struggling for more land as it is, without losing any.'

'So you risked your life over *land*?'

Something swirled between them—dark and tight—but she couldn't work it out.

'The government revoked the licence for eight months, maybe nine. But without it, Cesar and Therese only had about four vials of antivenom remaining and they couldn't acquire any more venom.'

'Someone told me that a nature programme presenter got bitten once and needed nineteen vials to keep him alive,' he bit out incredulously. 'Is that true?'

'Yes.'

'So then, how far did you really think four vials would go?'

'We didn't think about it,' she told him evenly. 'There was no choice, so we just got on with it.'

'You could have died.'

He doesn't care, she reminded herself urgently. *Don't read too much into it.*

'We could have.' She bowed her head, making no attempt to deny it. 'But we've all been bitten before—we build a little immunity. And, like I said, we had no choice.'

'You had a choice, Flávia. You all had a choice. You could have just kept yourself safe. Fought it in court and then gone back to the snakes when the government reissued the licences, or permits, or whatever.'

'To hundreds of dead or ill snakes? We had a responsibility to them, Jake. We weren't about to just abandon them.'

'You have a responsibility to yourself as well. And those who love you.'

'Now you really do sound like Enrico.'

She could actually feel the air around her turning frosty. Taut.

'Is that so?'

His tone was silky, and quiet. But she knew she didn't mistake the edge to it. And still she kept pushing the invisible boundaries.

'He didn't like me putting myself in danger, either. He always wanted me to give up the sanctuary part of my life and focus on working full-time from the research lab. As if the lab isn't the bit of my job that I endure until I can get back to the forest and escape the city.'

'Sounds very much as though he loved you,' he gritted out, scowling at her for so long that Flávia wondered if time had stood still.

'Maybe you're right,' she offered at length. 'At the time I didn't think so. I thought that if he really loved me, then he could never have asked me to choose.'

'And now you realised he cared and you regret your decision,' he scorned.

'No.' She pulled her lips together ruefully. And the way Jake's eyes followed the movement heated up her whole body. 'I guess the truth is that I just didn't love him back. At least not enough to want to give up my life for him.'

Something flickered across those morpho-blue pools. Too fast for her to follow.

'Maybe you just haven't met the right person yet,' he suggested.

'Is that an offer?' The wry question slipped off her lips before she could bite it back.

'That night was a one-off,' he answered hastily. 'I have Brady. My career is in the UK…'

'Relax.' She forced a laugh, and prayed it didn't sound as hollow to Jake's ears. 'I know you're not in the market for a relationship.'

'Evidently, neither are you.'

He paused, as though waiting to hear her response.

'No,' she answered, quelling the voice inside

which taunted otherwise. Assuring herself that the voice was wrong.

'I love my job. It's who I am. Surely, if someone loved me enough, he wouldn't ask me to change that?'

Jake didn't answer, though she wanted him to. More than she would have cared to admit.

She could imagine he was thinking about Brady, and how much the boy had already lost. And then, though she tried to pretend otherwise, she tried to imagine how he might feel if she and Jake were together and something happened to her.

And suddenly, she wondered if he'd lost more than he'd realised when Helen had died. She knew the rumours. She knew he'd always had a reputation for avoiding relationships, but now she'd gleaned the little she had about his parents, she couldn't help wondering if it had been a means of self-defence rather than anything else.

And had his sister's death affected him more than even he had realised?

'Perhaps you're right,' he murmured, as if feeling he ought to put an end to the conversation, but was unable to. 'But you're working on a venom-based therapy that could stop cancer cells from metastasising. That's incredible, Flávia. And you can still have that. You can still save all those lives. But do you have to be the one at the sanctuary risking your life to do it?'

'Yes,' she answered.

'Why?'

'Because, for me, it isn't just about the research to save human lives, Jake. It's about the protected habitats we're creating to save the snakes. It's about education for people not to club them to death—which you can understand when they know the snake could kill their kid within hours.'

Neither of them looked at each other, both of them appearing equally distracted by the to-ing and fro-ing of the barbecue guests. She wondered if his was as much of an act as hers.

'I need those snakes, Jake. I need to see them grow older, bigger, healthier, instead of seeing their numbers dwindle year on year. It's the only tangible reward I receive. I don't get to see the results in a patient, right there in front of me, telling me how I've changed their life.'

'But they're out there. More and more as each trial is successful.'

'Yes, and *you* get that. But I don't. I work in a lab and I work in the sanctuary. So the snakes are *my* patients. I shouldn't be told to give them up because it doesn't fit with someone else's idea of what I should reasonably do. How would you like it if someone told you that you couldn't be a surgeon any more?'

Jake opened his mouth to tell her it was completely different, but suddenly something stopped him. He wanted to argue, but he found that he could see what she was getting at.

Perhaps understand it. To a degree.

Even now, he still got a kick of satisfaction from being able to give a patient their life back. He got to see them, and their families, at that moment when they all realised that something he had done had given them the most precious gift of all.

The gift of time.

But Flávia, and others like her, never got that. Even though, without them, he couldn't do what he did.

So if she considered the snakes to be her patients, then he could understand why.

'You're right,' he answered eventually. 'I wouldn't like it if anyone asked me to give up what I do. Why should it be any different for you?'

She didn't answer out loud. Instead, she turned her head to look at him, scrutinise him, trying to decide whether he really meant it.

Then, after what felt like an age, she smiled. That soft, quirky smile of hers which seemed to have the knack of reverberating right through his gut and all the way along his sex.

One step and he could reach her, sweep her up

against him and carry her back into the house without any of the guests seeing.

God, what is wrong with me?

Gripping his drink tighter, he made himself take a long, deep swig.

'I've been watching Brady with Papai. And with the girls,' Flávia told him a few moments later. Oblivious to the battle he was waging with himself.

'Yeah?'

'The hospital isn't going to help Brady settle, you know. However lovely Patricia is, and whatever clubs they've laid on for the few kids who have come with their parents for this summer programme, it won't work for a boy like him. He won't be mentally and physically stimulated. He won't be happy.'

'No, I realise that. But I'll find a solution.'

'You could always bring him here for days out with Papai, or Maria, and even me. The girls like spending time with Brady.'

'That's incredibly thoughtful of you, but…'

'It's a longer commute for you, of course. But Luis makes it every day and he can show you the best routes.'

'I'm not bothered about me…but the imposition.'

'Papai loves taking the girls for walks and

teaching them new stuff. I know he'd love Brady's eagerness for learning.'

'That's incredibly kind, but you don't even know what your father or sister would think.'

'Of course I do,' Flávia scoffed immediately. 'Whose idea did you actually think it was?'

He didn't know what it was, but he couldn't help grinning. He might have known Flávia would push the credit onto someone else. Although, it was still ridiculously generous of her family to agree.

'It's really very—'

'Before you turn me down,' Flávia cut in, 'I should say that this has nothing to do with the other night. That was a one-off. Never to be repeated. It doesn't suit you because of Brady and it doesn't suit me because, frankly, I filled my fun quota for the year with you. Maria can't hassle me again for at least twelve months.'

Jake laughed.

It was amazing how he could have spent ten months not wanting to laugh at a single thing, and then Flávia had come along and in two encounters had brought light—*air*—back to his dark world.

'One more thing.' She finally pushed herself off the wall where she'd been lounging and spun around to face him.

It took everything he had not to haul her to him and take up where they'd left off a week ago.

'And what's that?' he asked, feigning an air of resignation.

'Before you decide, remember that this isn't about you, or me. This is about Brady. And what works best for that seven-year-old boy.'

Her amber eyes pierced through him. Pinning him down. So intelligent and so caring. But he thought he preferred them best when they were glazed over and spilling with need.

'I know this is about Brady.' Jake wasn't sure how he pulled himself together.

This staying away from her business wasn't really working. If anything, he thought it was making him want her more.

Maybe it was time for a differential diagnosis.

'I tell you what,' he answered thoughtfully, at last. 'I'll bring Brady here if you agree to come and watch a medical procedure with me.'

He saw her eyes flicker with interest before she even spoke.

'What kind of procedure?'

'The kind where I use one of the antivenoms we're trialling for VenomSci. One of the antivenoms that you helped to create.'

'You know, I have never actually seen one of those for real. Only footage afterwards. And I've followed case studies, of course.'

'You've never seen what we do close-up?'

'I worked tumour paint in the lab, but I was only a small part of that team, and then I moved on to my own project trying to find this application of snake venom to stop tumours from metastasising.'

'Nonetheless, you were still an integral part of the team that developed VenomSci's fluorescent dye. Want to see how you've helped to reshape the face of surgical oncology for me today?'

'You'd do that for me?'

'Why not?'

He knew he couldn't claim his offer was for entirely altruistic reasons. But when she looked at him like that, he didn't even care.

CHAPTER NINE

'THE FIRST THING I want to teach you is how to set up your camp correctly.'

'The first thing?' Jake answered dryly. 'You took my rucksack from me back at the house to give me one of your own instead. Then we spent the last few hours hacking our route through the jungle—and that was only after you instilled in me how crucial it is to have a machete and know how to wield it.'

Jake was glad his nephew was safe with Flávia's family. Only the prospect of a sleepover with his two new best friends, and the promise of a day on an adventure trail with Eduardo, had stopped Brady from kicking up a fuss about not accompanying Jake and Flávia into the Atlantic Forest.

'Are you pining for your luxury city life already, *urbanista*?' Flávia teased, the way she'd been doing more and more, ever since they'd left the city.

As though the rainforest was bringing out the real her, and she was more relaxed and contented than he'd ever known her. As though he was seeing the real Flávia, which very few others outside her family would ever see.

He found that he liked the sensation. Most likely a little too much. He could picture how it might be if this was the life he and Brady could lead for good. And then it worried him that it was all so easy to imagine.

No woman had ever made him think of the future before, not to mention that 'having fun for one night only' Flávia Maura certainly shouldn't be the one to break that pattern.

He had no room in his life for her. For any woman. He'd do well to remember that.

'You'd better believe I am. I simply don't see how you can prefer tramping through undergrowth, with no idea what lurks within, and eating corned beef hash out of a tin tray to the convenience of a hot power shower, climate control and a beautifully prepared meal.'

'Is that so?' She shook her head, smiling. 'Listen, Jake. Tell me what you hear.'

Jake listened, uncharacteristically obedient. This was her show. Her party.

'Nothing. I hear absolutely nothing,' he announced at length. 'No city buzz, no verve. No hooting of cars letting you know the place is full of energy. Alive.'

'Listen again.' She practically twirled round in

bliss, and he found his eyes drawn to the way her cargo pants perfectly cupped her pert backside.

You're in the jungle, for pity's sake.

'You can't hear all that you just described, it's true,' she continued, oblivious. 'But who wants to? All that noise pollution drowning out what really matters? You might not hear the loud city cacophony, Jake, but you can't say you can't hear anything. This place is practically teeming with life.'

He tore his gaze away and tried to listen again, a part of him loving the way her brow pulled taut in frustration at his admissions, making her look all the more adorable.

And tempting.

'The jungle is full of animals, and insects, all coming together in a harmonious concerto of sounds. Listen.' She closed her eyes and held her finger up as if to emphasise her point. And he tried. He really tried. 'I can hear birds, and frogs, and insects—all chirping, croaking, humming. I can even hear howler monkeys. And take in the scent of all that vegetation. Soil, wood, flowers, trees. It's as though the jungle is dancing with our every sense. Seducing them.'

Whatever innocent picture Flávia had succeeded in painting in his head shattered at that final comment.

All he could think about was a different kind

of seduction. The images in his head were all about Flávia, with that shimmering green dress of hers pooling at her feet, and that look of pure pleasure playing over her features. But Jake kept that to himself.

His body tightened at the memory, but he kept that to himself, too.

Instead, she continued.

'The reason I exchanged the rucksack you'd brought for one I'd packed myself is pretty much for this very reason.' There was almost a merriness to her tone. 'Bush craft is all about preparation. Working smart and planning out beforehand, so that ultimately you don't have to work harder than necessary. Especially out in the jungle when everything can be so unpredictable.'

'Go on, then, *jungle woman*,' he said softly. 'Give me your first lesson.'

She studied him sharply, but he could read that pulse flickering in her neck, and it didn't help his attempts to stay on topic.

She cleared her throat.

'When I'm setting up a temporary camp, I like the KISS approach…' She flushed but rushed on. 'As in, Keep It Simple.'

'Should I remind you that *kiss* is spelt with a double *S*?' he asked huskily, unable to empty his head of the image of his lips claiming hers.

'Fine.' Flávia glowered at him, but he noticed

the way she swallowed. Hard. 'Keep It Simple, Stupid.'

And what did it say about him that he liked how easily he could provoke her?

'In the top of your rucksack, you'll find a tarpaulin to shelter yourself from the rain, and a hammock to keep you off the jungle floor, each bound up with paracord. Get the tarp first…it's the camouflage one. Good. Wait—what are you doing?'

He stopped, looked.

'Don't leave your rucksack on the jungle floor like that—you'll get all manner of things trying to crawl in there and hitch a ride. Let me just tie this off…okay, you can hang it on that hook.'

The woman had a system for everything. And her bossiness was oddly compelling. He couldn't hardly help himself. What if he crossed the divide between them, his hands sliding around her waist, turning her to him?

'What about Raoul and Fabio?' he bit out.

'Don't worry about them,' Flávia answered merrily, her back still to him. 'They're over there making their own shelters from scratch. When you're done here, get them to show you how they strip vines to make ropes, and saplings like little joists.'

He looked around. Far away, but not far enough.

'They're building a damned house,' he exclaimed.

'More of a tree house, but I agree it's pretty impressive. Now, I chose this because it's a good spot. You have two fairly straight trees a decent distance apart over there, and two more just here. You're taller than me, so you take that pair over there.'

Dutifully, Jake ignored the protestations of his taut body and moved out to the farther set of trees, taking the bound-up tarp with him. He watched her smoothly unravel the cord from her own and began to copy. It didn't unravel quite so smoothly. Which might have been his lack of technique, or it might have been the fact that his mind was still elsewhere.

'Sorry.' She didn't make much of an effort to conceal her amusement. 'I tried to make it idiot-proof, but I guess I should have made it *urbanoid*-proof, too.'

'I'm glad I entertain you,' he remarked wryly.

'Okay, so loop it around one tree, as high up as you can reach, and tie it off using those knots we were practising with Brady the other night.' She deftly tied one of hers down to demonstrate, then stretched the line out and tied the other end off on the other tree.

Now, watching Flávia tie off another knot on another tree, Jake copied, possibly a little bit clumsily, yet bizarrely he wasn't hating the experience half as much as he'd feared he would. Especially when she crossed over to him to check his handiwork; the coconut scent of her hair, piled up on her head for practicality, pervaded his nostrils. His body went into overdrive yet again.

Good God, what the heck is it about this woman?

'Not bad.' She nodded. 'Not bad at all. Now, you need to open out the basher—the roof—and tie it off on some other trees. I have extra cord if you're missing a tree on one side and need me to make an extension.'

He looked around, trying to get a feel for it in his head, then set to work. Oddly, he was beginning to enjoy it. Whether it was because he could imagine teaching these skills to Brady or, more selfishly, because he enjoyed shaking Flávia's image of him as a city slicker, he didn't care to evaluate too deeply.

'Done,' he declared, looking up proudly. Where he had a roof—albeit a good one—she had a whole system in place, including a mosquito net, and what looked to be a hanging line for all her gear. 'My God, have you finished already?'

'I've been doing this a long time.' She laughed. 'Come on, we'll work together. You take one end of the mosquito net and I'll take the other. They can go below the tie-offs for the roof, but when you tie the tape ends of the hammock around the trees, they'll need to go above the cord for your net and your roof. Got it?'

'Got it,' he agreed.

It was incredible watching Flávia work. Like poetry. And he, who was accustomed to all manner of dexterous operations, might as well have been putting up his sleeping system with his thumbs and his toes.

But then, suddenly, it was done. A roof, a mosquito net and a hammock, all complete.

'Okay, here's some extra cord. You can tie that off up near the apex of your tarp, but inside the mosquito net, then you can hang your gear off that during the night and nothing will get in there. And whilst you do that, I'm going to try and find some dry firewood so that we can light a fire.'

'Using what? Two sticks?' he teased.

Flávia arched her eyebrows at him.

'I can, if I really need to. But I'm usually more organised than that, urbanoid. I carry a lighter and a few strips of rubber. That gets a fire started pretty nicely, even if the firewood is wet, as it so often is in the forest.'

'Then what?'

'Then you cook me dinner,' she told him happily, grabbing her machete and heading into the jungle.

He lifted his head.

'What are we supposed to eat?'

'Rat,' she called over her shoulder. 'I'll hunt them, you'll cook.'

And he was left staring at her in disbelief as she plunged into the undergrowth, her sexy posterior practically wiggling at him as she moved.

In the end, she had lit a fire, taken a small pan from out of her rucksack and a couple of sealed ration packs, and they'd eaten a pre-prepared meal. But it had occurred to Jake that this prank-style Flávia was a different Flávia again from either the one with her family, or the one at the hospital.

And it had sent a bizarre sense of possessiveness through him that he seemed to be the only person—at least outside of her family—to see this side of her. Another layer to his fierce, strong *selvagem*.

The real Flávia Maura.

And when she looked at him, and laughed as though he was the only man in the world, he'd had to contend with a great fire roaring through his veins, proclaiming things it had no right to as he looked at her.

Mine. Only mine.

And telling himself it was sheer insanity did nothing to dampen the flames. They'd only been fanned the more she'd opened up her world to him. As though letting him in to another universe inside of her that no one else ever got to experience.

It felt inevitable that something more would happen—needed to happen—between them. He felt the inexorable draw and, rather than fight it, he found himself welcoming it.

Flávia was like no one else he'd ever known. Even here, and now, he knew he'd never meet anyone like her ever again.

They'd even been onto Fabio and Raoul's tree house with Raoul's high-tech camera and seen some of the jungle's nocturnal creatures, including a crab-eating fox, a prehensile-tailed porcupine and a fight between a wandering spider and a raid of army ants.

'Brady would go mad for this,' Jake had said in awe.

And so Flávia had given such vivid detail to each and every one of them, things that he could pass on to his sponge-like nephew, that he'd found himself lost in her passion. More and more, he could see what she saw in Brady that he had missed all these months.

It didn't make him feel good.

Now, lying in his hammock, in the relative dark with nothing but the sounds of the jungle around them, and the crackling of the fire, it felt almost intimate. Raoul and Fabio were close enough for safety but not so close that they could hear any conversation he and Flávia might have.

And right now, he was glad of it, because he was still grappling with the questions running around his head.

'A penny for your thoughts,' she said softly. 'I think that's the phrase?'

He shouldn't answer, and yet Jake found himself opening his mouth. As if he was the kind of man who found it that easy to talk.

Except, with Flávia, he was turning into that man. And he couldn't help but think that it wasn't a bad thing.

'I think I'm beginning to understand Brady's obsess...*fascination*,' he corrected, 'for this stuff. Just like you.'

'Just like me,' she concurred quietly.

'I wouldn't have seen it, if you hadn't come along.'

He knew he would never have made the admission back in so-called real life. But here, now, he could say it to the stunning, starry night sky—a sky like none he'd ever seen before. The lack of light pollution, just as Flávia had said.

And he could say it to Flávia.

'I think you would have.' He could hear the soft smile even in her voice. 'It just might have taken you a bit longer, and you wouldn't have known what you were looking for.'

'I want to believe it. But I'm afraid, in this, that view affords me too much credit.'

'Then look at it this way. You'll never have to find out because, fortunately, you *do* know. Even better, you're acting on it.'

'I still don't know whether to bring him out here.'

'He'd love it,' Flávia laughed softly.

'Oh, he would. No question. But I still don't know if it's responsible to bring a seven-year-old into the Atlantic Forest.'

The air went silent, though not still, as Flávia appeared to ponder his question.

'Many kids, maybe not,' she offered eventually. 'Although, they do run mini expeditions from the city and there are kids under ten. But Brady is different. He would really soak it all in.'

'I know, but—'

'You're not his father, but you're wholly responsible for him,' she supplied. 'Which makes the decision that much harder.'

He blew out a deep breath and time passed, but he didn't know how long.

Maybe a lifetime.

He'd never voiced these fears to anyone before. He didn't even know he was going to voice them to Flávia, until he heard them coming out of his mouth.

'I don't know about any of that. I just know that

I made a promise to Helen that I would take care of Brady, and I would never break that promise. But… I can't reach Brady. I can't connect with him. He doesn't seem to notice whether I'm there or not and I don't know that I'm the right person to bring out the best in another human being.'

He didn't mention the fact that *love* wasn't even an emotion he was sure he possessed. At least, not in that all-consuming way that parents had for their kids. Or even couples had for each other. Because the fact was that the more time he and Brady spent with Flávia and her family, the more he began to wonder if maybe he *could* learn to love after all.

The way Helen had believed he would. And the way Flávia had told him he could.

'I know he was close with his mother. He was Helen's little prince. But I can't seem to build a relationship with him and I feel he is withdrawing every month that goes by. Then I try to make amends by letting him get away with behaviour that I know school would pull him up over. I don't want to be so poor of a guardian to my nephew that I actually end up somehow damaging him.'

He didn't know what he expected Flávia to say; he certainly wasn't expecting her to say something which would make him feel instantly better. So why was he so compelled to talk to her?

Either way, she was silent for so long that Jake began to regret voicing the plaguing doubts.

'It's an impossible balance,' she conceded. 'Maria makes it look so easy, but it isn't. Kids do need boundaries, though. They have to know their limits. But have you talked to Brady about his mother since that day in the visitor centre?'

'I tried...' Jake thought back. 'I asked him if he missed her, but he didn't respond.'

Certainly not the way he had with Flávia when he'd broken down in her arms. And he hadn't pushed. Who would *want* to make a child cry, anyway?

She tilted her head. 'Maybe there's another way to approach it.'

'Go on,' he encouraged when she fell quiet. The crackling of the fire was almost a comforting sound in the noises of the jungle.

'Maybe instead of asking him about his feelings, you should tell him about yours, first.'

'Talk to him about my...*feelings*?' Jake blew out sharply.

'It isn't a dirty word,' she chided gently.

'I know that. I just... What would I even say?'

'I don't know—tell him some of the good things you remember about his mother.'

'I didn't even know Helen these last ten years. What would I tell Brady?'

'Then tell him about your memories of her as

a kid. She told Brady you were once a good big brother to her—can't you talk about that?'

'I don't even know how I was a good brother.' Jake shook his head in the darkness, and he wondered if she could hear the same ring of anger to it that he could. 'I guess I was just...*there*... someone to talk to about what was going on in our lives. Not that we did all that much, but God knows our parents *never* talked to us about anything other than homework, or school, or something equally educational.'

'You once said they did their duty by you?'

And Jake didn't expect himself to answer; this was far too personal for his liking. Yet he heard himself speak, all the same.

'They were academic surgeons. High-achieving, focused, but detached. If they weren't learning on a practical level, they were writing medical papers, securing research funding, travelling the world for conferences. They sent Helen and me to good schools, dressed us in new clothes and kept a clean, albeit old-fashioned home. They believed there was nothing my sister and I couldn't learn from books.'

She didn't answer, but he knew she was listening. Absorbing it all.

'They provided for us well, but they were detached. Cold. You could go to them for practical, medicinal care if you were ill, but forget a show of affection, or a word of love. That wasn't who they were.'

'I can't imagine that,' Flávia said quietly, and he could well believe it having met her sister and her father, who had given him an exuberant bear hug the first time he'd met him at that family barbecue.

'You've seen how I am.' Jake shrugged. 'I never really thought anything was lacking. Until Brady came along.'

'I think you did,' Flávia countered after a moment. 'You just didn't have any reason to tackle it. But his mother wasn't like that, clearly.'

'No,' he agreed. 'Somehow, Helen managed to change things for herself. For Brady. I don't know how.'

'Why did you fall out?'

'We didn't.' He shrugged, scarcely able to believe he was still talking. Still confiding about things he had barely even let himself *think* about in the past. 'We just…drifted apart when we went to uni.'

'To study medicine,' Flávia finished, more as if she was thinking out loud than actually talking to him.

'What is it you want to know?' he asked astutely.

'I suppose—' her answer was slow, thoughtful

'—that a part of me wonders why you followed them into medicine. Given how they were.'

As though she knew him better than anyone else ever had.

'Not just medicine. Surgery. They didn't want doctors for kids… They insisted we both became surgeons.'

'Insisted?' He could actually hear the smile in her voice, could imagine it hovering on her lips, as if she didn't fully believe him.

He didn't blame her.

'There was no option. They made it clear from as early an age as I can remember that they would never accept anything else from either of us but becoming surgeons.'

'Oh.'

'Actually, I didn't want to,' he shocked himself by saying. 'I spent most of my childhood and teenage years dreaming of becoming an engineer.'

It was a confession he'd never told a living soul.

The moment seemed to hang between them.

'It should surprise me more,' she murmured after a while. 'You're such a skilled, driven, compassionate surgeon, it's no wonder you were sought out to run clinical trials. But the truth is that it doesn't surprise me that much at all.'

'I don't know if that's a compliment.'

'It is,' she laughed softly. 'So you and your sister are…were…both surgeons.'

'I am. Well, you know that, of course. But although Helen studied medicine at uni, it was partway through her third year that she fell pregnant with Brady.'

'I can't imagine that went down well, from everything you've said.'

'It didn't,' he acknowledged. 'They didn't shout, or yell—that wasn't their style. But they told her that she was too young, that a baby would ruin her career at this stage and that the logical solution was to terminate.'

He could remember it now. The cool, firm statement made as they'd all sat around the table in a restaurant for a typically uptight *family meal*. There had been no scene in any real sense of the word.

'What happened?' Flávia asked tentatively, drawing him back to the present.

'Helen wiped her mouth with her napkin, set it to one side and quietly told them that she would be keeping her baby. Then she got up and discreetly walked out of the restaurant.'

Not that her parents had ever made any attempt to stop her.

'And that was it?'

'That was it. They went back to their lives, I went back to uni and Helen did her own thing.

We didn't see her again for about six years. So, you see, I wasn't much of a brother to her at all.'

'What about the father? If you don't mind me asking.'

And the fact was that he didn't. He had no idea why he was still talking—maybe it was the intimacy the rainforest created—but it was somehow cathartic.

'Helen never told us who he was. The first and only time I met Brady he was five, and I did ask her about the father. But she simply said that she'd told him she was pregnant and given him the choice of how involved he wanted to be. Apparently, she'd never heard from him again, but her son was her world.'

'I can tell that. She was a good mum.'

'She was,' Jake agreed. 'I've no idea how, given the example we had set for us. I just know that whatever she had, I don't have it in me. But I'm trying, thanks to you, and I should be grateful for that much.'

He'd possibly intended the conversation to end there, but he heard the light creaking of the tree and could imagine she was flipping onto her side on her hammock. When she spoke, her sweet, gentle voice seemed that little bit closer.

Or perhaps that was just his wishful thinking.

'It's up to you, Jake. You can be as close as you want to. The question of whether you bring him into the jungle or not is more about the symptom than the cure. If you want that connection, then yes, you just need to approach Brady like he's more than a seven-year-old kid. And yes, you need to talk to him, ask him what he wants. But more than that, I should imagine, you need to talk to him about his mother. Because you're the only connection he has left to her now.'

'Maybe you're right—when we get back to the city, I'll take him out for something to eat and we'll talk.'

'One more night after this one and then you talk. *Really* talk,' Flávia added fiercely, the second greatest champion Brady had ever had.

As though she truly cares, Jake thought as he stared past the confines of his shelter roof, and to the vast night sky beyond.

CHAPTER TEN

FLÁVIA HURRIED INTO Maria and Luis's pool house, and froze.

She'd intended to drop off large towels whilst Jake was filling Brady in on the two days of their short jungle expedition. Either that, or Brady would have been filling Jake in on his first ever sleepover in her sister's mad household.

She hadn't expected to be faced with the sheer mouthwatering sight of Jake standing in the kitchen with only a tiny towel around his waist, his dark hair still slick from the shower.

'Where's Brady?' she managed, her tongue suddenly too thick for her mouth.

'Maria took them all out for ice cream. Apparently, she'd promised them this morning and she hadn't expected us back until much later.'

'Oh. Right.'

'She made a point of telling me that they wouldn't be back for a few hours.'

'Oh,' Flávia repeated. Then, as the import of his words sank in, she felt the flush creep up her body. *'Oh.'*

'She isn't the most subtle, your sister.' Jake grinned suddenly.

'No. Not at all. Anyway, I… I thought you might need these,' she offered redundantly, edging forward to slide the towels onto a bar stool before edging backwards again.

But only a few steps, her body resisting all instructions from her brain to turn around and leave.

The revelations of two nights ago had been more than she'd expected, and at times she'd even convinced herself that there was something arcing between them again. She'd even been waiting—hoping—for something to happen out there. A loaded glance, maybe. Or even a stolen kiss. But ultimately, nothing had happened.

She'd told herself it was for the best. That her… dalliance with Jake had been over after that one night together and now she was just trying to be a good friend to him. And to Brady. But right now Jake was standing metres from her, practically naked, his lightly tanned skin shimmering from the water. Worse, with a hungry gleam in his eye that seemed to perfectly match the roar inside her.

Try as she might, it was impossible to stop her eyes from skimming their way down his body. From the sharp lines of his jaw, over the impossibly contoured ridges of his abdomen and to the deep V which disappeared tantalisingly below the fluffy, white material.

She didn't want to be his friend. She wanted more than that.

And she wanted it too much.

Flávia swallowed. Once. Twice. Dragged her eyes back up to where they ought to be. But they didn't quite make it, and instead she found herself staring at some point around his collarbone, forcing her mouth into more mundane conversation.

'I thought you'd still be telling Brady about your *jungle adventure*, as he calls it.'

'Brady said he'd rather hear about it when you're there.' The wry smile was almost her undoing. 'He thinks I might miss important fauna details.'

Flávia tried to laugh, but it came out slightly choked. Her heartbeat was frantic. Her skin felt like it was too tight for her own body, and between her legs was molten.

'You *will* need to get the details right.'

'Don't I know it?' He flashed her a smile which felt like it was shot through with lust, and the air thickened in the room around them.

She ought to leave. The door was right behind her. But she still couldn't seem to get her feet moving.

'Do you want a drink?' She didn't even realise she'd started moving again until she found herself in the kitchen area. 'There should be something in the fridge.'

Then she was standing in front of him, so close that she could imagine reaching her hands out to flatten them against those oh-so-appealing abdominal muscles. Her palms prickled with the effort of resisting. And then she lifted her head, their gazes colliding, his eyes hot, and almost black with desire.

It was like a catalyst.

Jake slid one hand into her hair—still wet from her own shower—and hauled her to him, his head bowing so that his mouth could claim hers and at last—*at last*—they were kissing again.

Only, Jake didn't merely kiss her, he dominated her. Deliciously and devastatingly so. Even better than she remembered.

His mouth claimed hers with such complete authority, just as electrifying as she remembered. She could feel it deep in her core.

A heat bloomed right through Flávia.

She pressed her body against his, her hands gliding over him and revelling in every ridge and every dip, as though she couldn't get enough. Her entire body shivered when he dipped his fingers into the waistband of her jeans and hooked around her fitted white tee, pulling it up and over her head.

Then Jake unhooked her bra and removed that,

too, her nipples proud as they strained against his chest. The slide of her bare skin over his was almost too delicious, and as he kissed a trail along her jawline and down her neck, his hand skimmed over her to cup one heavy, aching breast.

Gentle and demanding all at once, driving the sense of anticipation up even further.

Almost too much to stand.

He toyed with her, played with her, then let his hands smooth over her skin as if reacquainting himself with every inch of her. From the ridges of her spine to the soft curve of her waist. Only, unlike last time, this felt less urgent.

More indulgent.

Without thinking, Flávia reached out and hooked one finger into the waistband of his towel and it fell away with one flick.

Her mouth went dry in an instant. She hadn't overplayed her memories of last time as she'd begun to fear she might have, because he was every bit as hard, ready and uncompromisingly masculine as she recalled.

She didn't realise he'd swept her into his arms, high against his chest, until he started carrying her through to the bedroom, and all she could do was cling tightly and gaze at him, lost in those impossibly blue depths.

A thrill coursed through Flávia as he laid her on the bed, and stripped her down with ruthless efficiency. She sank back, expecting him to move alongside her, to cover her body with his own, but suddenly she felt his hands slide under her backside and pull her forward.

When she looked up, he had already settled himself between her legs, a wicked curve to his lips, and her heart slammed against her ribs.

'Jake…'

'Brace yourself, my *selvagem*. Now it's time for me to dole out the lessons.'

Before she could answer, he lowered his head and used his tongue to trace the line up the inside of her raised thigh only to stop a breath short of her core. Then he tracked his way back down the other thigh.

It was the sweetest torment she thought she'd ever known.

Again and again he teased her, stoking her desire, making her lift her hips in anticipation each time, only for him to skim over where she needed him most. She threaded her fingers through his hair, unable to help herself.

'Anyone would think you didn't know how to hit your mark,' she grumbled breathlessly on his third time over.

'Oh, I know how to hit my mark,' he muttered, his mouth never leaving her skin. So close that she could feel the curve of his wicked smile. 'You just don't know how to ask for it nicely.'

She lifted her head to glare at him, but this time, when he reached the top, he paused, and looked at her.

'Still, maybe I should prove it to you.'

Then he dipped his head and licked his way into her. Jettisoning her into pure sensation.

He tasted her, over and over, using his tongue like the most exquisite weapon against her. Licking her, sucking her and making that hot thing in her belly pull tighter, more hectic.

She rode them out for as long as she could, these desperately perfect sensations. And when she didn't think she could bear it any longer, he sucked harder and slid one finger deep inside her.

Flávia broke apart. Splintering into a million tiny fragments which she didn't think she'd ever be able to put back together. No one had ever made her feel like this. So wanton. So alive.

By the time Flávia came back to herself, it was to find Jake lying next to her, propped on one arm and watching her, his expression entirely too self-satisfied for her liking. She'd been entirely too lost in the moment and she felt the flush of embarrassment creeping over her.

'That was hardly balanced.' She was going for prim, but her raspy voice fell far too short of the mark.

'You aren't really complaining.'

Less of a question, more of a statement.

Unable to answer, she merely reached for him, pulling him onto her. Letting him haul her into his arms beneath him, and settling himself between her legs like he was meant to be there.

And, so help her, that yearning in her swirled around all the more. Coiling tighter every time he nudged against her entrance, making her want to lose herself all over again. Not that she could, surely? Not so soon?'

Flávia shifted her hips, trying to find out, and a low sound escaped the back of Jake's throat.

'Careful, Flávia,' he warned.

Could it be that he wasn't as in control as he was pretending to be?

The realisation stirred through her. She tried it again with the same result. Lifting her legs, Flávia wrapped them, with deliberate ease, around Jake's hips and wriggled around him.

'If you keep doing that, I'm not going to be responsible, my *selvagem*,' he growled.

She felt heady, too close to the edge. Again. Already.

'Who says I want you to?' she murmured, meeting his eyes as he looked at her.

Then he held her gaze as he thrust into her. Long, and slow, and deep, as her lungs expelled every last bit of air in a soft, juddering sigh, before drawing back out again.

'Again,' she choked out, her arms looped around his neck and her legs still locked around his waist. And he complied with devastating control once. Twice.

Each time, she could feel herself adjust to him, tighten around him, and then he started to set the pace. Steadily at first, but building quickly, the fire raging wildly under every inch of her skin. And Flávia, already halfway there from what he'd already done with her oh-so-compliant body, clutched tightly and surrendered to him.

In. Out. Faster and faster, taking her higher than she'd ever been, until he was driving her straight to the edge, and her body was shaking as she begged him not to stop.

Never to stop.

So good that she could almost cry.

When he slid his hand down between them, it was like a ball of flames shooting straight through her veins, and he finally took her over the edge.

For one long moment, she felt herself floating there, and there was nothing but a white heat rushing headlong towards her. And then it hit, and she started falling—spinning and somersaulting over and over as she tumbled into the blissful abyss, calling Jake's name.

And as he followed her, this time he called her name, too.

* * *

By the time she woke, several hours later, she was alone in the bed.

She glanced around for Jake, even listening out for the sound of him moving around in the main lounge, but it was silent out there. Of course, he would have had to take Brady home. She'd lost track of time, but he couldn't afford to. Their lives were so very different.

Sitting up, Flávia threw her feet over the edge of the bed and moved gingerly forward. Her body ached in places which hadn't ached for too long; they'd been intimate twice more after that first time. But, crucially, it was her heart which ached the most.

She glanced tentatively around the bedroom—the supposed scene of the crime—but even though she had no idea how Jake was going to treat her the next time she saw him, she couldn't say that she regretted what had happened.

Scanning further, she'd been surprised, even touched, to see her clothes folded over the chair in the corner of the room rather than dropped around the place as they'd left them. But then it occurred to her that he hadn't done it for her, but to ensure than Brady didn't see anything when they'd all returned home after their ice-cream trip.

Quickly, she grabbed a shower—Jake had

thought to place the towels she'd brought in the bathroom—and dressed, before hurrying out to the main house. And straight into her sister, who eyed her knowingly.

'Good afternoon?'

'Great,' Flávia replied loftily. 'And yours?'

'Well, I got honeycomb ice cream, so I can't complain.'

Flávia waited for Maria to say anything more. Unreasonably disappointed when she didn't.

'Did you…um…see Jake before he left?'

'Well, now that you come to mention it, I do believe I did.'

Another pause. It seemed that her sister was going to make her fish for every detail.

'And did he say anything?'

Maria cocked her head speculatively.

'Livvy…'

'Uh-oh.' Flávia forced herself to grin. 'I know that tone—it's never a good one.'

'No.' Maria shook her head. 'It's not like that.'

'Then what?'

'You're not falling for this guy, are you?'

'Of course not,' Flávia scoffed. But even to her own ears her voice was too bright. Too high.

'Oh, *Livvy*.'

'I'm not.'

'This is all my fault.' Maria shook her head, her hand reaching out to stroke Flávia's cheek.

Flávia pulled away sharply. 'I'm *not* falling for Jake. You told me to have a little fun, that night of the gala, remember? So that's what I'm doing. I'm having a little fun.'

'You're falling for him.'

'No,' Flávia denied.

Only in that instant she realised, with blinding clarity, that she was lying.

'You can't fall for him, Livvy. He's leaving. In a matter of weeks,' Maria pointed out forcefully.

'I know that.'

So why did it now press so heavily on her chest that she felt as though she was suffocating?'

'Do you? Because I've never seen you like... *this* before, Livvy.' Maria swirled her arm in Flávia's general direction. 'Not even with Enrico. And if I'm right, then you're setting yourself up for the hardest fall of your life.'

'You're wrong.' Flávia crossed her arms obstinately. 'I know the situation. Jake is going back to England, and I'm going back to the jungle.'

'And he *will* be going, Livvy.'

'I know, Maria.' Flávia rolled her eyes. 'Look, it was only supposed to be a bit of fun that night. But then this happened—and do I need to remind you that *you're* the one who encouraged it, with your "we won't be back for hours" comment? But that's it now.'

'I encouraged you before I realised you were in so deep,' Maria censored.

'Well, I'm not. Look, I've had fun, but now it's done. I doubt I'll even see Jake again before the closing dinner.'

'Is that right?' Her sister pulled a suspicious face.

'It is,' Flávia concluded firmly.

'Well, you won't care that he asked you to meet him tomorrow, then.'

As bait went, it was a powerful one. Flávia felt her heart stop. Then lurch. She glared at Maria, who looked equally defiant.

'Meet where?' she demanded.

'What does it matter?'

'Maria?'

Okay, so she was in deeper than even she had realised. But she knew there was a deadline to their relationship.

Jake *would* be leaving. And as long as she remembered that, she could certainly handle anything else.

'Where does he want me to meet him, Maria?'

Maria pursed her lips and then finally relented.

'For breakfast, at the café opposite Paulista's.'

'When?'

'About seven.'

Flávia drew in a breath and tried to rein in the galloping in her chest.

'Thank you,' she told her sister at last.

'Livvy—'

'I know,' she cut her sister off, moderating it with as gentle a smile as she could manage. 'I'll be careful.'

Only, Flávia had a feeling she was already further gone than she would ever have wanted to be. Yet, she couldn't bring herself to care.

CHAPTER ELEVEN

'DID YOU TELL your uncle what you saw on the adventure trail yesterday?' Flávia asked Brady as he finished his eggs and sat back, replete.

Brady wrinkled his nose.

'Uncle Jake isn't like us. He doesn't like animals—he only likes his hospital work.'

There was no animosity in the boy's tone, no making a point, just a simple statement of fact. Which arguably made it all the more damning an indictment, as though for every three steps forward he seemed to be making with his nephew, they then took two steps backwards.

But before Jake could say anything, Flávia cut in, her voice light and encouraging.

'I think he'd be really interested to hear about the otter Maria told me you saw, though.'

Brady didn't look convinced. He just turned his head, and Jake could only categorise his expression as *wary*. It cut, deeper than Jake might have thought.

Over Brady's head, Flávia was dipping her head, clearly suggesting he say something. Jake wasn't certain what that something was, so he took a guess.

'I really would like to hear,' he managed, and her rewarding smile really shouldn't have made him feel quite so proud. Like a kid in class getting a coveted gold star from the teacher. Nonetheless, it emboldened him. 'Mate?'

Jake wasn't sure what he'd expected. Whether he'd thought perhaps that Brady would see right through his feeble attempt to connect, and scorn him for it. Or had he just thought that Brady would refuse to respond?

Too little, too late.

Either way, it wasn't the flash of pleasure which shot through the boy's eyes, dissipating the first little bit of wariness.

'Really?'

'Sure.' He made himself smile at his nephew. It wasn't that hard.

'Okay, we saw a neotropical otter—or *lontra longicaudis.*'

'Wow.' Jake nodded enthusiastically, hoping it was the appropriate response.

A triumphant grin pushed a little more of the wariness off Brady's face.

'It's amazing, isn't it? The neotropical otter is on the "threatened" list in the *Red List* of endangered Brazilian fauna.'

'I did not know that,' Jake answered, relieved that he hadn't simply offered to take Jake to the zoo the moment they got home to see the otters there.

'They usually avoid areas with high human traffic—it disturbs them.' Brady was warming up to the topic now. 'But they like high riverbanks to avoid floor issues, and lots of vegetation to provide coverage and protection.'

'I see.'

Was his chest actually swelling at hearing the happiness in his nephew's voice? The passion? The way that Flávia did when she talked about the rainforest. Or the way that he felt about his own career.

How had he missed this in Brady before? How had he dismissed the boy as a kid who had nothing really relevant to say? No wonder he hadn't been able to connect with Brady.

If it hadn't been for Flávia, he might never have seen a possible way to do so now.

If it wasn't too late.

He could imagine his sister talking to Brady one to one. Taking him on her own version of Eduardo's adventure trail. Helen had always been more like Flávia's family than like their own detached parents. Than like himself.

'Want to know what we saw in the jungle?' Flávia opened her eyes wide, her voice already painting a picture that had Brady spinning around in anticipation.

'What?'

And then his nephew's gaze turned on him as Flávia glanced over Brady's head expectantly, and Jake felt lost all over again.

'What did you see?' Brady repeated.

'We saw a Brazilian wandering spider.'

'Wow!' Brady breathed, awestruck.

'But there's something even more incredible, isn't there, Jake?'

Realisation hit him. Hard.

'Oh, no,' he balked. 'I really don't think a seven-year-old—'

'I do,' Flávia cut in firmly. 'I *really* do. Trust me, he's a boy. But first, Brady, can you tell me anything about the Brazilian wandering spider?'

'Well.' He frowned, deep in thought. 'They're quite big spiders. Brown and hairy, and they're called wandering spiders because they don't build webs like other spiders, but they hide under logs and stuff in the day, and then at night they come out and wander the jungle floor looking for prey.'

'Do you know what they eat?' she asked.

'Um…insects? Mice? Maybe other spiders?'

'Right.' Flávia nodded. 'Know what other insects come out at night? I'll give you a clue— they build living fortresses, known as bivouacs.'

'Army ants!' Brady shouted out.

'Well done, mate,' Jake praised as Flávia gesticulated wildly over his head. 'So, did you know that army ants send out thousands of ants at a time to hunt prey?'

'Yes.' Brady eyed him, unimpressed. 'They're called raids. And by the way, there are about two hundred subspecies of army ants.'

'Well, we saw army ants and a wandering spider come face-to-face.'

'Wow!' Jake had hoped to capture Brady's interest, but he hadn't been prepared for the level of attention his nephew was now directing at him. 'Did they battle? Who won? Was it incredible?'

'Ultimately, the spider—'

'We'd love to hear who you think might win a battle like that,' Flávia cut in swiftly, and belatedly Jake realized he needed to prolong the moment, and get himself and Brady to engage with each other on a level that his nephew would love.

'Hmm.' Brady knitted his forehead together. 'Well, I think that the army ants are fearless and fierce. They can inject venom to paralyse their prey using a stinger, and they have sharp mandibles which cut insects and crush them. They could tear the legs off the spider.'

'Yeah, we saw how ruthless they are.' Jake nodded, trusting that Flávia knew what she was doing and it wasn't going to give Brady nightmares.

Then again, with everything he'd been learning about the boy lately, he was beginning to realise that whilst the human world may hold painful experiences for his nephew, Brady could cope far better with the concept of survival in the natural world.

'The wandering spider has the most potent venom of any spider, though. It even kills humans. The spider would have to win over the ants, wouldn't it?'

'Yeah, I thought that, too,' Jake agreed. 'But actually, when we watched, we saw the sheer number of ants overcome the spider, and they ended up taking it down within minutes.'

'That's so cool,' Brady enthused. 'I wish I could have seen that. Can you take me into the jungle next time, Uncle Jake? Please? I know Flávia will look after us.'

Jake hesitated. He wanted to agree, especially because he was starting to understand why it meant so much to the kid. But he needed time. He wouldn't be rushed into it. The objective was to bond with Brady, true; it had to be the responsible thing to do. And right now, he couldn't be certain that agreeing wasn't just him leaping at the opportunity to spend more time with Flávia.

With each day that passed, his return to London got closer, and yet with each moment spent with Flávia, it was getting harder and harder to imagine his old life back in the UK.

He didn't *want* to imagine it. And he knew, without Brady even having to say a word, that his nephew felt the same. Which was, ironically, some sort of progress.

But Jake couldn't shake the ridiculous notion that progress meant nothing without that one, unique woman.

He felt tied up in one of her friction hitch knots. He knew there was an easy release, but if he pulled the wrong way he'd end up bound tighter than ever.

'I honestly don't know, mate,' he answered, and this time, it didn't feel so odd using the nickname. 'I can't promise you that we will, but I can promise you that I will seriously think about it.'

And even though Brady sulked, he realised that he didn't feel as guilty, or as lost, as he might have done in the past. He was setting appropriate boundaries and he was sticking with them, the way Flávia had told him he ought to do.

He noticed that Flávia was deliberately staying out of it, and he was grateful for her tact, even if a part of him wondered if she would have handled it differently.

But then, to Jake's surprise, Brady's sulk lasted only a few seconds before he bit his lip and seemed to pull himself together.

'I'm sorry, Uncle Jake,' he managed, delving into his bag and pulling out a sheet of paper. 'Vovô Eduardo says he doesn't like sulking. And

Julianna says that I look like a baby. So I want to give you this.'

He looked down and saw the bird picture and it was as though someone had sat on his chest. It felt tight. Or full. Or both. Brady had never given him anything before, let alone one of his precious wildlife drawings.

This one was yellow and black, and whilst it might not be artist quality, it was nonetheless an impressive representation.

'It's a saffron-cowled blackbird,' Brady qualified.

'It's really…very beautiful,' Jake managed.

He tried to add something more but suddenly found it was impossible. His chest was swelling even more, and there was an unfamiliar ball lodged in his throat. It was almost a relief that Brady was turning to Flávia, his cheeks suddenly flushed, looking apologetic.

'I was going to draw it for you,' he mumbled an apology. 'But I just thought that Uncle Jake might like it… Maybe for his office?'

'I think it's a really lovely gesture,' she assured him, taking Brady's chin in her hand and dazzling him with her brightest, most beautiful smile.

And Jake thought he was the only one who heard the slight thickness to her voice.

'I'll hang it on the wall for all my patients to see,' Jake managed brightly at last, his chest now constricted, as though it couldn't make up its mind how to feel.

Whatever he'd expected from this summer programme in Brazil, however he'd imagined it going medical-wise, he had never, in his wildest dreams, thought that it might improve his fractured relationship with his nephew. And he knew he had Flávia to thank for that.

'Come out with me,' he announced abruptly, the moment Brady had left to look for something—Jake realised belatedly that he hadn't even been paying attention.

'Sorry?'

Startled amber eyes flickered to his and something deep inside Jake shifted, and burned.

He had no idea what he was doing. In a couple of weeks, he and Brady would be gone. Back to England. Back to normal life. And yet here he was, proposing dates as though any relationship between him and Flávia actually had a future.

It was nonsensical. And still, he waited impatiently for her answer.

'You're taking me to the Theatro Municipal de São Paulo?' she guessed the moment he ushered her off the subway.

'I am,' he confirmed. 'You were born in this city, yet Maria told me that you haven't been since you were about six.'

'It wasn't the rainforest,' she quipped. 'So you can hold your shock.'

She hadn't intended to sound so sharp, but it was almost touching that he'd planned this out. Certainly, it was more than she'd been expecting, as if this…non-thing between them was more than just sex, and more than just Brady.

Just like yesterday morning, sitting in that café sharing breakfast with Jake and Brady. He was sharing more and more with her, first offering her glimpses of the secrets he held inside his head, and then almost inviting her in.

It was intoxicating to feel as though she was some kind of confidante to him. The *only* confidante he'd ever had. And it all felt so remarkably right. So easy.

Yet, wasn't that what made it all the more dangerous?

It made her let her own guard down, and let him in. It made her forget that he would be leaving soon, but when she remembered, pain slammed into her, hard and painful. And given that she'd known the situation from the start, it had no right to do so.

No right whatsoever, a voice shouted loudly inside her head.

Only, it didn't sound as angry as it was trying to. It just sounded frightened and lost, which made no sense. Everything should just go back to the way it had been before they met. Except that a part of her couldn't even remember what that had been.

Didn't want to.

'I'm sorry,' she apologised. 'I didn't mean it like that. It's a lovely thought for a date. Really.'

Jake didn't answer; instead he brushed a stray hair from her face and tucked it behind her ear. Excruciatingly tenderly. It was all she could do not to tilt her head and lean her cheek into the warmth of his palm.

'I think you'll love it, so trust me, okay?'

She nodded wordlessly. The insane part was that she did trust him.

Then, taking her hand in what felt like a ridiculously intimate gesture, he pulled her body into his and they walked along the street together until they turned the corner and the stone steps and glorious pillars of the *theatro* came into view.

They stood for a moment, drinking in the stunning architecture, until Flávia turned and realised he had been studying her instead.

'Did I tell you how beautiful you look tonight?'

'Thank you.'

She lowered her head, knowing she was blushing, but hardly even caring. With any other man, she might have been wary that it was a line. A thing to say. But she was quickly realising that, with Jake, he was too serious and too direct to feed a person lines.

If he told her she looked beautiful, it was because he thought she did. And because he said it, she didn't let herself worry that she looked like some wild jungle creature. She simply believed him.

It should have rung an orchestra of alarm bells in her head. The summer programme was nearly over and he would be leaving soon. Letting herself get attached could only end in heartache. And yet, she was letting herself do precisely that.

Just as if a part of her hoped she might be able to change the inevitable by sheer power of thought.

If she had any sense, she would turn around and tell Jake Cooper that she was happy to be his colleague, his friend, but that this date could never lead anywhere.

Better still, she would make her excuses, turn around and leave. Back to her family, and her career, and all the things she could depend on.

'Ready?' he asked, holding out his arm.

And then, because she'd always been drawn to the most dangerous flames, Flávia turned her head to cast him her brightest smile, and she took his arm.

'I loved that,' Flávia exclaimed a couple of hours later as they exited their floor of the *theatro* and headed down one side of the sweeping, double staircase. 'I didn't think I would, but I did. So thank you.'

'Such faith.' Jake shook his head. 'This way.'

'Where are we going now?'

'Another surprise,' he told her. 'I'm glad you liked the theatre. Maria told me you used to love this place when you all came here as a family. I guess I hoped it would bring back those happy memories.'

'I don't know about that, but I know it has created new happy memories, which stand strong all on their own.'

'Are they that sad?' he asked abruptly, the odd expression on her face gnawing into him. 'Is that how you knew I needed to create positive memories with Brady so that he had some which didn't all involve Helen?'

'It's slightly different.' She shot him a smile, but it was too bright, too brittle, for Jake's liking. 'His mum died.'

'As did yours.' He frowned.

Flávia stopped. She twisted her head around to look at him.

'What made you think that?'

'You told me you understood exactly how he felt. You said that.'

'I said I understood how he felt with regards to

his passion for nature, and science. I never said my mum died.'

'But she did, didn't she?'

The silence was so leaden, so oppressive, that Jake was sure he'd stopped even breathing.

'My mum didn't die,' Flávia gritted out when he'd almost given up hope of her speaking. 'She walked out. Leaving my father to pick up the pieces for two devastated little girls.'

A complication of emotions twisted their way across her lovely face at that moment, and Jake wished he could take back every word. To have never reminded her of such pain. For the conversation never to have started.

But it had, and he needed to find a way through it.

'Do you want to talk?'

'No.' Then, 'Maybe.

'My mother had never wanted to be a mother. She was a nurse, but I think she'd always wished she could have been a doctor.'

'Why wasn't she?'

'I don't know. I don't think she ever wanted to have children, but then she met my father, fell pregnant and got married. She became a wife and mother and that was what her family expected of her. And as long as she moulded to those rules, everything was acceptable. The fact that she made a terrible mother seemed to be something everyone was prepared to overlook.'

He couldn't explain what it was that made him want to…to *be there* for her.

'Terrible, how?'

She wrinkled her nose and pulled her lips together as though she didn't want to be telling him any of this, and yet somehow couldn't help herself.

'You once told me that your parents didn't neglect you. They gave you time—as long as it was the topics they deemed important—but they didn't show you emotion. Well, my mother *did* neglect us.'

'You and Maria?' Jake asked gently as Flávia swallowed.

'Right. My…our…mother only ever really acknowledged us if it gave her a way to blow off some steam, you know, vent her frustrations? And I gave her plenty of excuses to do so.'

'You?'

Flávia shrugged, as though trying to ward off the terrible memories.

'My sister told you I got into fights in school, right? Ironically, I hated the fights at home so I would constantly sneak out of the house. I'd just creep into the edges of the forest so that I could see the animals, and I'd stay there for hours watching them. It infuriated my mother.'

'Could she perhaps have been concerned?' Jake

asked carefully. He, of all people, knew better than to sit in judgement. 'Frightened for you?'

Flávia's mouth twisted into a hollow smile that tugged at his chest.

'A part of me wishes that were true. But no, her only concern was for the hassle that I brought. She would shout at me. *Scream* at me. Always saying how much she hated me.'

'Flávia...' He couldn't imagine anyone hating someone as bright, and interested, and sweet, as her.

'She was always telling me that I made her life difficult,' Flávia continued, clearly trying to keep her voice level. Even succeeding at times. 'That I was impossible. And I believed it, for years. It was only when I grew up that I realised my transgressions were just excuses for her to shout at me. The real truth was that she hated me for existing in the first place. Maria, too.'

'Flávia, I'm so sorry. I had no idea. But you know that was more about her than about you. You understand that now, don't you? She isn't worth your time or your heart now.'

'I know that,' she agreed, her eyes locking with his, searching them. And when some of the tension eased from her face, he couldn't help but wonder if that was because of him. 'Although, Maria did track her down a few years ago. I didn't want anything to do with her, but Maria had just had Julianna and Marcie and she needed to understand what had driven our mother to be the way she was.'

'Why?'

Flávia twisted her face again.

'I don't know. My best guess is that she was afraid of turning out like her. She wanted to be sure.'

This time it was more of a grimace, and Jake felt his heart fracture at the expression. He didn't know what to say, or what to do.

'The worst thing about it was that she had remarried, only a couple of years after she'd walked out on us. And despite everything she'd said, she'd had another family with him.'

'Flávia,' he muttered, pulling her to him and cradling her in his arms.

He stroked her hair as if that single action could somehow make all her pain go away.

It was beginning to explain a lot. Like why she loved escaping into the rainforest, or how she focused on her work. Even why she kept people at bay.

Except for Brady.

And maybe himself.

'I swore I would never be like her, Jake. I promised myself I wouldn't make those mistakes. I wouldn't drag a family into the kind of life that I lead. Yet, I inserted myself into your life, yours and Brady's, and I had no right.'

'And we're both so much better off for you in it.'

Which sounded a hell of a lot like a declaration that he hadn't even known he wanted to make.

It was insane. Preposterous. And it couldn't happen. In a matter of weeks, the summer programme would be over and he and Brady would be flying back to the UK. There was no doubt in Jake's mind that the next sensible action, the reasonable one, would be to start creating some much-needed distance from this quirky, funny, sexy woman who had, incredibly, managed to sneak under his skin.

For his sake, but mainly for Brady's. Because God knew they were both at greater risk than ever of falling for the unique Flávia Maura.

Which only made his next move all the more irrational.

'If that offer to take us into the rainforest is still on, I think when I get my free weekend next week, Brady and I would very much like to take you up on it.'

'You trust me?' She stared up at him, her amber eyes bright, proud. 'With Brady?'

'There's no one else I'd trust more,' he assured her, lowering his head and finally, *finally*, claiming her mouth with his.

CHAPTER TWELVE

'*PARE! OLHE!*'

Raoul stopped abruptly, pointing something out that Flávia had to train her eyes for a moment to see.

'Wait,' she instructed Brady and Jake in turn, then panned with her camera until it caught what Raoul had first spotted. 'Look—there in that glory bush.'

Brady and Jake peered into the image and belatedly, Flávia realised that she had effectively invited Jake to step closer to her. As her thundering heartbeat now heralded.

The past few hours with Jake had been eased by the presence of both Brady and Raoul. She'd used the pair of them almost as a shield to help her create some distance from Jake.

It had to be one of the hardest things she'd ever had to do in her life, but what choice did she have?

Flávia didn't even recognise the woman she'd been last week on their date. She had never opened up to anyone—not even Maria—the way she'd opened up to Jake. It went deeper than the mere secrets she'd shared with him. It was more than just the way his grey-blue eyes had seemed to shine light on the darker corners of her soul, making the things which had once scared her seem less frightening. It had gone beyond the way they'd returned to her city apartment and made love slowly and tenderly. Then hard and illicitly.

And for the first time in her life, her apartment had felt like a home instead of just the crash pad she used when she couldn't get back to the rain-forest and it was too late to travel to Maria's.

That entire night with Jake had felt like a surrender.

And it terrified her.

So, she'd gone out of her way to avoid bumping into him ever since. She'd snuck in and out of her lab and avoided all the places in the hospital that she knew he usually frequented. She'd even avoided Brady—which only made her feel guilt on top of all these other tumbling, confusing emotions.

It had been fortunate that the week had also been one of the busiest of the summer training programme and she'd known Jake had practically been in back-to-back teaching operations and seminars, anyway.

So why didn't she feel that fortunate?

But now she was here, in the middle of the Atlantic Forest with Jake, and it was getting harder and harder to pretend things were normal between them. She had no idea what he was thinking, and it was making her crazy.

She was turning herself inside out. Wondering. Imagining. And then, trying to act as though it didn't matter to her.

Impossible.

'Wow…' Brady breathed, drawing her back to the present in an instant.

And as soon as he did, her gaze pulled inexorably to Jake. Just in time to watch as his eyebrows knitted together in disbelief.

Her fingers actually ached to reach out and smooth his brow.

Hopeless!

'What *is* that?' The scepticism leapt from his tone. 'It can't be real.'

'It's real.' Flávia ignored her leaping nerves and tried for a light laugh. 'Even though, I'll agree, it looks like something straight out of a sci-fi movie. Gentlemen, meet *bocydium globulare*—aka the Brazilian treehopper.'

'No, surely not? That's really real?' Jake shook his head.

'What are the balls on its head?' Brady demanded, fascinated.

And she found it was easier to concentrate on Brady and pretend that Jake wasn't there.

'Ah, now, they are spheres of chitin, a fibrous substance and primary component of the exoskeletons of arthropods, as well as the cell walls of fungi.'

Brady touched the screen with his finger, as though it could somehow bring him closer.

'Is it a male?'

'Nice guess—you might think so given how flamboyant the males of species often are compared to their female counterparts,' Flávia congratulated. 'But actually, this ornamentation is found on both sexes of treehopper alike.'

'So what are the spheres for?' Brady asked.

'Honestly, Brady, we're not entirely sure. We think it's possible that they are there to deter predators. It would certainly be harder to catch and eat something like this with all those balls on its head, wouldn't it?'

'Yeah.' Brady nodded vigorously.

'That said,' Flávia hurried on, reminding herself to stay focused on Brady rather than the fact that Jake seemed to have taken a step closer and was now sending her reactions into overdrive, 'these spherical ornaments also sport bristles, so it's possible that they are sensory bristles and the ornamentation also has some tactile function we don't yet understand.'

'That's so cool,' Brady inhaled.

'I like to think so.'

It was all she could do not to snap the camera

back into place and leap away from Jake. To try to regain even a fracture of her composure.

Her brain didn't really seem to be functioning well all of a sudden.

'Anyway, come on, the sanctuary is this way.'

'I didn't know we were going to the sanctuary?' Jake frowned, his low voice sending ripples right through her.

'We weren't.' Why was it suddenly so hard to keep her voice light, and breezy? 'But I thought you might like to see it, given the amount I've talked about it.'

And maybe there she could remind herself where her heart, and mind, lay. And help her to get over this obsession with a man who could never exist in her real world.

'Flávia...'

She wanted so badly to stop. To talk to him.

Pretending not to hear, Flávia practically launched herself in front of Raoul. Anything to establish a bit of a gap—however artificial—between her and Jake.

'Come on. I'll lead the way for a bit.'

Cesar stepped into the designated habitat, the large viper coiled on the ground, and Flávia watched him move his homemade staff to the snake's neck. Gentle and accurate, that was Cesar's motto. And much as the two of them adored their beloved snakes, they would never lose respect for what the powerful animals were capable of.

She held her breath, as she always did at these moments. Then Cesar was moving, fast and precise, pinning the bushmaster to the ground before scooping it up, keeping its neck straight and smooth so it couldn't snap its head back and clamping it under his arm.

Flávia moved forward quickly with the film-covered container, and Cesar lowered the snake until it bit down, its venom sliding into the clear pot.

'I always hate this bit,' he muttered, his accent as heavy as ever. 'But I have to tell myself that every sample is a step closer to finding a solution that will make my countrymen realise how valuable these snakes can be and therefore encourage them to cherish the animals instead of merely fearing them.'

Carefully placing the pot in another, sealed container, Flávia exited the cage and handed it off to Raoul, who promptly turned to Brady, who had been waiting outside in safety, with Jake. The passionate little boy appeared to have captured yet another heart.

'Come,' Raoul said to Brady and Jake, 'I show you where this goes now.'

'This is amazing,' the young boy enthused.

'I'm going to make a project as soon as I get back home.'

'To the UK?' Raoul guessed. 'Are you looking forward to it?'

Brady's face darkened instantly.

'No, I don't like it there.'

'Excuse me,' apologised Raoul hastily. 'I was thinking...'

He tailed off but it didn't matter. Brady hadn't taken offence. He never did.

'I meant home to where Vovô Eduardo is. And Julianna and Marcie.'

'Ah...' Raoul looked over Brady's head with a knowing smile. 'Flávia's family are being very kind. I, too, am liking them very much.'

'I wish I could stay with them for ever. I don't want to go back to England next week.'

Next week!

As Flávia went hot, then cold, she watched Jake stiffen, and in that moment she would have given anything to know what was going on in his head.

It didn't matter how much she'd been reminding herself of the truth, and schooling herself to keep her distance; the truth sounded that much less palatable when she heard it spoken aloud.

She couldn't speak. Couldn't even breathe. All she could do was stand, motionless, watching as Raoul led Brady and Jake out. Pretending she wasn't standing there, staring at the door long after they'd left, and it had slammed shut behind them.

Why had Jake reacted? Because he didn't want to be leaving in a week's time? Or because, for him, it couldn't come soon enough?

She was desperate to know.

But worse, she was terrified that he might give her the wrong answer.

'Ready to get more samples?' Cesar's voice at her shoulder made her jump.

'Yes.' She snapped sharply back into the present. In this job, there was no time to be distracted. 'Ready.'

For the next half hour they worked quickly and systematically, collecting sample after sample, and packing them away carefully. She fought to focus, using the space as a chance to remind herself what really mattered in her life. Her career, and her snakes. Not some fling who seemed to have got inside her head, however much he felt like more than that.

What really mattered was her work with Cesar. With VenomSci. And slowly, slowly, she managed to calm her racing heart and throw herself into the task she knew so well. They worked steadily, going from enclosure to enclosure and collecting venom from each bushmaster, treating the snakes with care but always respecting them.

By the time they had finished and made their

way back through the sanctuary, Jake was sitting at the battered old picnic bench in the staff area and being treated to Raoul's homemade dessert using the most succulent exotic fruits.

'Where's Brady?'

'Fabio took him to look at something snake-related.' Jake shrugged.

'So you guys are leaving next week.' She tried for upbeat and breezy as she slid in opposite Jake.

It had been the little test she'd set for herself as she'd been working. And she'd passed. But now it was getting harder as she sat there whilst Jake studied her for a long moment.

'Brady wouldn't be, if he could get his way. Your sister would be ending up with a third kid all of a sudden. And not the baby she keeps teasing Luis that she's going to have.'

She tried to echo his low laugh, wondering if it was just her imagination that it sounded more forced than usual.

'I honestly don't think Maria would mind. She's rather taken with Brady. They all are.'

'You're very lucky, Flávia. You have an incredible family, and you're so close.'

'Yes.' She swallowed abruptly. 'Well, we've had to be.'

'Because of your mother,' he said softly.

And she hated that he could read her thoughts.

Hated, she repeated firmly. Not *loved* the fact that he seemed to understand her so well.

But that didn't mean she needed to bore Jake with the details of her own childhood sadness. Her mother walking out wasn't exactly in the realms of what had happened to Brady's mum, but it had affected her all the same. It had moulded the person she was—as Enrico had pointed out, *very* categorically.

'Never mind.' She shut down the discussion quickly, her own fault for such a thoughtless comment in the first place, of course.

Still, she shook off the melancholy that seemed to be hovering; she was where she needed to be now, so she was more than happy with the way her life had turned out.

At least, she had been, until Jake had slammed into it and apparently knocked it off its comfortable little axis. And try as she might, she couldn't seem to restore order.

'So what about you? Are you looking forward to leaving? Getting back to your own hospital and your work?'

He took a fraction longer than necessary responding.

'I *will* enjoy getting back to my own hospital. Maybe implanting some of the lessons learned here.'

It wasn't exactly the answer she'd been hoping

for. She plastered the brightest smile on her face and forced out a hollow laugh.

'Lovely. That's fabulous.'

'It is?' he asked softly, not joining in with her brittle laughter.

Yet she couldn't bring herself to stop.

'Well, of course. Isn't it?'

And when he looked at her like he was in that instant, his blue eyes almost silver, it was enough to make her stomach twist itself up into the most perfect Siberian hitch knot.

'I don't know,' he answered softly. 'Can we talk?'

'Talk?' she echoed weakly.

A hundred questions tumbled through her head. A thousand. But all Flávia could do was nod jerkily, before a commotion by the door caught her attention and a few words made their way to her ears.

Government inspection?

'We have to go now,' Cesar confirmed. 'Flávia, are you coming?'

'Coming,' she responded instantly, steadfastly ignoring the regret that washed over her.

This was her job. It had to come first.

She shot an apologetic glance to Jake, who wore a disconcertingly neutral expression. If he was disappointed not to have had that conversation, then he wasn't showing it. Then she followed Cesar out the door.

And if an odd sense of foreboding followed her, then she refused to let it affect her.

Jake knew something was wrong even before anyone uttered the words. Even before people started rushing around in a frenzy.

He couldn't have said how he knew or, more to the point, he didn't want to acknowledge how. That icy wash that poured through his veins with no warning, and for no apparent reason, an hour later.

'*Acidente*. Accident,' Raoul growled as he raced by.

'What kind of accident?' Jake demanded. 'Where's Brady?'

'He's fine—he's with Fabio.' But Jake couldn't shake the sick feeling in his stomach as he fell in behind the running Raoul. 'Flávia?'

He knew.

'Flávia? *Sim*. Flávia is collecting *o veneno*. Venom.'

'She was bitten?' He yanked open the door to the medical room, all but pushing Raoul ahead of him with the medical supplies.

'*Sim*. Yes. The *idiota* government official—he go into enclosure because he see no snake. Flávia, she try to stop him. She get the bites.'

An overwhelming sense of horror swept through him. Filling every last dark corner and jagged crevice inside of him. Snuffing out all the little atoms of light she had begun to leave there.

He'd never known anyone like Flávia. The thought of losing her was almost too much to withstand. Following Raoul, they entered where Cesar had Flávia on a table.

'Is she okay?' His tongue felt too thick for his mouth, his lips numb.

This was why he didn't do emotion. This was why he'd carried on the harsh lessons having parents like his had taught him, and kept himself detached.

Because he had no doubt that he had never felt worse than he did, right at this moment.

'No.' Cesar looked up, his face grim, his eyes flashing with a combination of fear and fury as he took the supplies from Raoul.

Disastrously, it was the fear that seemed to be winning out. Though he knew Cesar would never succumb to it.

'Antivenom,' Cesar demanded urgently, all but snatching the vials that Raoul presented to him. 'I can't stabilise her blood pressure.'

Jake advanced into the room, his eyes trained on Flávia.

'What can I do?'

'I need to administer an initial bolus dose of AVS, and immobilise the affected lower limb.'

'You deal with the limb, I'll get an intravenous catheter for the AVS.' He quickly picked up the kit he needed.

The medical bit was something he could do eyes closed. And it made him feel as though he was *acting* instead of simply watching. Dreading.

Jake efficiently inserted the catheter so the AVS could be administered continually, before checking the bandages Cesar had applied. They were tight, but not so tight that they threatened too-tight arterial compression.

'Good,' he muttered, stepping forward to perform a fresh set of obs.

'We have called *ambulância aérea*?' Cesar asked.

'Air ambulance?' Jake nodded and looked towards Raoul. 'They're on their way?'

'Sim.'

That was good, at least.

'You will travel with Flávia?' Cesar asked Jake quietly.

He wanted to say yes. He'd never wanted something so much in his life. Flávia looked so small, so fragile, that something in Jake's chest seem to crack wide open. He could hardly bear to see her there. But he had Brady to think about.

Not just in this moment, something nagged at him. *But for life.*

'No,' he ground out. 'You must go. You know more about the snake that bit her. I'll get Raoul and Fabio to lead Brady and me back out.'

He barely waited for Cesar to agree before he resumed his continual monitoring of Flávia— checking her vitals, making sure she was still alive—and with each moment that ticked by, the reality of the situation rammed home inside him and words scraped against the roof of his mouth, paring away at it.

This wasn't something he'd ever thought he could, or would, say to anyone. But he needed to say it. Here. Now.

He covered her smooth hand with his, before sliding his other hand beneath it, too. As though he could protect her from every possible storm, when the real truth was that he couldn't protect her from anything, because Flávia Maura *was* that storm.

And he told her that she was a glorious, wild, terrifying monsoon. And that he...*loved* her for it. If this flawed, terrifying thing he felt could even be called *love*.

Although if it was love, his voice cracked at that point, *how would he even know?*

Abruptly, Cesar's radio crackled into life and a voice alerted him to the fact that the *ambulância aérea* had arrived. And Jake stepped back, waiting for them to come through the doors.

It was just over twelve hours later when Flávia stirred from sleep in her hospital bed as the doctor came in to check on her. Jake's neck was killing him from the awkward position he'd been sleeping in in the wingback chair, but he didn't care.

Maria and Eduardo were still asleep—Maria on the couch, and Eduardo in a similar straight-backed chair. They had only dropped off around three in the morning, and he was loath to wake them, but he knew they wouldn't miss this moment for a second.

He tried to follow as the doctor chatted with Flávia, and from Maria's tearful laugh and vigorous nodding, and Eduardo looking slightly less pale than before, it seemed to be good news. He clenched his hands in his pockets; it had never been this hard to be patient before, but they'd been good enough letting him join them in the room. The least he could do would be to bite his tongue.

Still, it felt like an eternity before the doctor left and his heart lifted a fraction more as he watched Maria and Eduardo hug each other, then Flávia, then each other again. And then they both hugged him.

'We're going for breakfast,' Maria told him, patting his arm. 'Give Flávia a chance to tell you…the news.'

He waited for them to leave before crossing the room. Lowering his head, he stroked her hair and planted a soft kiss on her forehead.

'I take it it's good news, then?'

'There's some localised swelling and oedema, and they want to keep me in a bit longer for observation, but the preliminary assessment is that I am going to be all right.'

'That's good,' he managed. It was impossible to articulate how relieved he felt. Nonetheless, his mind was whirling. 'How is that even possible?'

'They can't say for certain, but there are a few theories. First off, it was a very young bushmaster. Also, it didn't deliver the kind of bite that I know it could have. And because I've been bitten so many times during my career—not just by bushmasters, but by other snakes, by spiders, bullet ants, there's quite a list—my body has built up some immunity to toxins. Enough that, when combined with the antivenom I received, and the fact that it was administered so quickly, I seem to be remarkably *okay.*'

'So there won't be any long-term effects?'

For an instant, he thought she hesitated, as though there was something more to say, but then she smiled. A tight, tired smile, but a smile nonetheless.

It had to be just his edginess which had him seeing things that weren't really there.

'They won't know for certain until all the test results come back,' Flávia told him, and this time he was sure her voice sounded odd. Strained. 'But as I said, preliminary findings look good.'

He wasn't sure he could take her lying to him.

'Is there something you aren't saying?' he bit out.

She hesitated again.

'Is it true that you were in that room with Cesar? That you took charge like it was one of your operations?'

'Anyone would have,' he managed gruffly.

'I remember hearing certain things…' she managed after a while. 'At least, I think I did. It's kind of hazy.'

It took him a moment to realise that it was a question.

'What did you hear?' he demanded, his voice clipped.

She flushed, and he knew what she was going to say.

'Something about me being…a monsoon? And—' she stopped, her cheeks flushing even darker before she dropped her voice to little more than a whisper '—and that you love me?'

'I also said I don't even know what love is,' he rasped. 'And it doesn't matter either way.'

'I think you do,' she began before pausing. Frowning. 'What do you mean it doesn't matter?'

He would have given anything to wipe away the wary look that had just clouded her beautiful features.

Instead, Jake thought of Brady, and he slammed a steel cage shut around his chest. And whatever it was that might, or might not, be inside it.

'It doesn't matter because I can't be with you.'

He heard her sharp intake of breath. Saw her pale. But he couldn't cede. Not now. There was more than just him and her to think about.

'You don't understand…' she began helplessly, but he cut her off.

'I think I do,' he said. 'You once told me that you love your job, that it's who you are. And you said that if a person loved you enough, they wouldn't ask you to change that.'

'I remember,' she managed.

'Well, I'm not asking you to change. I know who you are and I accept that.'

'Jake…'

'But I can't be with you. I can't put Brady through what I went through today. I *won't*.'

He ignored the sharp lance of pain, just as he shut his ears to the taunting voice, needling that maybe it wasn't just Brady he wanted to spare from the pain of today.

That maybe he himself couldn't stand to go through it again.

But he refused to ask her to change who she was. That would be like finding a bird of paradise, only to clip its wings to prevent it from flying. And Flávia deserved to fly.

He just couldn't stand to watch her get too close to the sun.

'I see,' she managed at last.

And he thought the brittleness of her voice might topple him once and for all.

'Well, listen, Jake. Thanks for being here, but you really shouldn't.'

'I don't have to go right this second,' he told her gruffly, a tightness lodged in his throat. A huge part of him madly wanting to claw every word back.

Wishing things were different. And he'd never been the kind of man to wish for things that couldn't be.

'I can stay. Until you're on your feet,' he rasped. 'In fact, right now there's nowhere else I'd rather be.'

For a fraction of a second, her whole face appeared to soften and threatened to crumple. He moved in, on some insane whim, to kiss it smooth, but Flávia turned her head and seemed to steel herself, right before his eyes.

'But there's somewhere else *I* would rather you were.'

'Sorry?' He wasn't sure he was following her.

Again, she hesitated, as if she was having second thoughts. Or perhaps that was just his imagination.

Everything in him was spinning. Sliding this way and that as though it didn't know where it was meant to be.

'This is a time I should have my family around me,' she said firmly. Pointedly. 'And you have your own family to care for.'

He'd hurt her. He hadn't wanted to, but what choice was there? It was her or Brady. Still, it didn't mean he found it that easy to turn his back on her. Not when every fibre of his being was howling at him to change his mind. To find a way to make it work.

'Brady is with Luis,' he managed. 'And Julianna and Marcie.'

'But he should be with *you*,' she answered, and he felt the barb as surely as if she'd jabbed it into his skin.

'You want me to go now,' he realised.

He could hardly blame her after all he'd just said, so this was no time to succumb to this offensive, putrid *thing* sloshing around inside him.

'Message understood.' He stood. Stiffly. Awkwardly. 'I should have thought. I won't disturb you any longer.'

'Jake…' she whispered, looking suddenly pained. 'It's just…you're right. It wouldn't be fair on Brady, for a start. That kid has been through enough with his mother without having to deal with…*this*.'

She was grasping. Making excuses. He could read her as easily as he could read an X-ray.

My God, does she actually pity me?

'Don't concern yourself,' he managed flatly. 'As you so unambiguously put it, Brady is my family, my responsibility. Not yours.'

Even though he'd made his decision, his heart still cracked when he thought about trying to explain to Brady why he wouldn't be seeing Flávia, or Maria, ever again. To say nothing of Eduardo, or the girls. But Flávia was right—it was better that than his young nephew ever seeing Flávia like this. Or worse.

Jake had managed to whisk Brady home from the forest with the quiet assistance of Fabio without panicking him about what had happened to Flávia. The official line was that she'd been called away for a government inspection and that was it. He could never bear to tell the boy that something had happened to her.

He wasn't sure he would ever be able to bear

hearing it himself. Which only seemed to confirm that it wasn't just Brady's heart he was trying to protect.

Not that he cared to dwell on that particular realisation right now.

CHAPTER THIRTEEN

'FOR THE LAST TIME, Livvy, will you just call the guy and tell him how you feel? Before you dust the paint off my favourite vases?'

Miles away, her sister's voice finally penetrated Flávia's subconscious and she looked up from her cleaning task. She lurched forward, knocked a vase, steadied it and stared at Maria loftily.

'I don't know what you're talking about.'

Maria rolled her eyes.

'Of course you do. You've been moping around for the last month. Ever since Jake and Brady left for England.'

So much for thinking that she'd contained her feelings well. Still, Flávia pulled back her shoulders and thrust her head a little higher into the air.

But it was exhausting, trying to pretend that her heart wasn't smashed into a billion tiny fragments.

She should never have sent Jake away. *Never.* But what choice had she had? Once the doctor had told her the news.

'Should I remind you that I got bitten? That I've been unwell? If I have been acting a little oddly, it's because I'm under the weather. Not because I'm *moping*!' She practically spat the word out.

Maria levelled a direct stare at her. 'You've been moping.'

'No, I—'

'You love the guy and he loves you. So why make a drama out of it when all you have to do is call him and tell him you're sorry?' she added archly.

'I don't love him,' Flávia protested—poorly, probably, since this was to her sister. She felt too hot. Too...*tight*. 'But even if I did, Jake Cooper certainly doesn't love me.'

'He loves you. And if you explain why you lied, he may just understand and still love you.'

It was foolish, the spark of hope that danced inside her chest. Moreover, it was dangerous.

'I didn't lie, I just omitted one detail. And only because they still had no idea at that time what would happen, given the bite,' she parroted out the excuse she'd been telling herself ever since that morning.

'You lied,' Maria stated flatly. 'And you know it.'

Flávia began to deny, then thought better. She rubbed her hands over her eyes.

'It's more complicated than that.'

'Only if you make it more complicated.'

'No.' She shook her head at her sister, her

shoulders starting to slump as the fight left her. 'You're right. He talked to me about love, but when I got bitten he realised that he couldn't be with me. He couldn't put Brady through that if next time I wasn't as lucky. If next time, the bite is fatal.'

'Couldn't put Brady through it, or himself?' Maria wondered, more to herself than to Flávia.

Either way, Flávia's pulse kicked up a notch. Had she wanted Maria to argue the point? Somehow?

'Turns out Jake isn't so different from Enrico.'

'He's completely different,' her sister refuted instantly. 'And I know you know that, too.'

'How? How is it different, Maria?' cried Flávia. 'They both ultimately needed me to give up my snakes, my career, to be with them.'

'Not your career, just the dangerous part. The same bit that you yourself have talked about giving up ever since you found out about the baby. You need to call Jake, Livvy.'

'Call him and say what?' Flávia lifted her hand and dropped it against her thigh in despair. 'That I'm pregnant, but whilst I seem to be okay, the doctors still have no idea how the bite might have affected the baby?'

'It's a start.'

'Right,' she snorted, but it was more like fear, regret and grief all merging into one harsh sound.

'So, get Jake to drop everything and drag Brady halfway across the world for a baby that might not even survive.'

'I think Jake would rather prefer that to being left in the dark, the way he is now,' Maria pointed out, not unkindly.

'I don't think he would,' Flávia countered defiantly, as if that could somehow quell her jangling nerves.

Frankly, she had no idea what Jake thought. She wasn't sure she had ever really known. Though her sister didn't need to know that.

'I'm telling you, when it comes down to it, there are no differences between Jake and Enrico.'

'There are lots of differences.'

'Go on, then. Give me one of them.'

She hadn't realised how desperately she wanted to make that distinction until she levelled the question at her sister.

'I'll give you two,' Maria replied. 'First, Enrico gave you an ultimatum a year after he'd already asked you to marry him. Mainly because you didn't exactly rush to set a date, and deep down he knew that you weren't as eager to marry him as he was to marry you.'

'I loved him,' Flávia lied.

'No, you didn't, and you know that. You're just being obstinate now. You would never have gone to the lengths for him that you went to for Jake these past few months.'

'I was looking out for Brady, his seven-year-old nephew,' Flávia pointed out hotly as something swelled up inside her.

Something she couldn't—or didn't want to— yet identify.

'You were,' Maria agreed with a delicate lift of one shoulder. 'But you were also doing it for Jake.'

'And the second difference?' Flávia demanded.

For a moment, her sister just watched her. Studied her.

'The second difference is you, Livvy,' she said at last. 'It's how you feel about each man. You could never have contemplated changing any part of what you do for Enrico. But your heart hasn't been in it at all since Jake left. *That's* your main difference.'

'It's my career, my life, and I love what I do.'

She always had loved it. So why didn't it hold quite the same power that it had before?

'I know that,' Maria acknowledged. 'But we both know you're going to change it, anyway. For your baby. Besides, no one is saying give up your career completely.'

'Then, what?' Flávia asked.

Her head was a mess from all the back and

forth. If only she knew what she really thought. What Jake really thought.

'You can keep doing your work in the sanctuary, and you can raise awareness. Just give up going into the pits for the collections. You said Cesar was thinking about doing so because he was getting old and his grip was weakening. Isn't that why Fabio and Raoul have been drafted in? To start taking on that side of it? And there are two other employees now, aren't there?'

'Yes.'

'So, there you go. You ease back on the hands-on, just like Cesar is. But no one's asking you to give up the sanctuary altogether, Livvy. We all know it's part of who you are, and what you love.'

And it was odd, wasn't it, that the suggestion didn't fill her with indignation, like it would have even two months ago. But still, something bubbled away inside her. Low yet lethal.

She tried to articulate it, but the words wouldn't come.

'What if I'm not cut out for it?' she settled for instead. 'What if I give it up for him, for the baby, and then I end up resenting him for it?'

'You won't.'

She almost envied Maria her certainty, because her own fears were starting to eat away inside her.

'You can't know that.'

'I can.'

'How?'

And the beat hung between them for such an interminably long moment.

'Because you're not our mother,' Maria said quietly. Angrily.

Everything around Flávia started to spin, and it was impossible to keep the pleading from her voice. All this time, she'd thought Maria hadn't known her deepest fears.

'How can you be so sure?' she whispered.

'Because I am. Because you're a completely different person than her. You're a loyal sister, a loving aunt and a compassionate woman. You love your job, but you didn't put it ahead of your family... Well, sometimes you did, but nothing like the way that she did.'

And despite everything, they both laughed, albeit weakly.

'You're not like *her*, Livvy. You never were. But especially not now.'

Flávia didn't know how long they stood together, whilst she absorbed what her sister was telling her. She might look tough but deep down she wasn't, she never had been, and right now she didn't even feel herself. She felt stripped down, fragile, broken. Just like the delicate back of her beloved bushmasters.

But finally, finally, she lifted her eyes and looked at Maria.

'So I decide to do that…to throttle back on the hands-on work at the sanctuary. Then what?' And there was no way she could keep the shake from her voice.

'Then you call Jake and set out what you've decided, and you tell him that you love him.'

'I don't know. That's a scary idea.'

'Scary?' Maria laughed. 'Telling him you love him is scary? You got bitten, several times over the years, and yet you went back in with those bushmasters of yours each time. Surely, *that's* scary?'

'Not if Jake walks away from me. He already has done once.'

'Because you sent him away.' Maria blew out a deep breath. 'I don't know, that's just my two cents' worth. But ultimately, Flávia, it's down to you.'

And the words echoed through Flávia's head all afternoon and all the way home.

Ultimately, it was down to her.

Jake leaned on his car as the kids were let out of school, waiting at a distance the way that Brady had asked him to do. Still, he didn't miss the march from the building, or the tightly locked jaw.

'How was your day?'

'Three words,' Brady bit out mutinously as he

practically threw himself into the vehicle. 'Brazil. Right. Now.'

Each word was punctuated by the little lad counting a finger in mid-air. The worst of it was Jake couldn't agree more. But he couldn't say that; it was his job to make his nephew feel better.

'Listen, mate,' he offered, 'I'm sorry that it was a bad day, but— '

'I want to go home.'

'This *is* home...'

'No. Home was in São Paulo. I miss those weekends in the rainforest,' Brady cut in, his eyes locking with Jake's in challenge. 'I miss Julianna and Marcie, and Vovô Eduardo. And I miss Maria and Luis. Most of all, I miss Flávia.'

'I miss Flávia, too, mate,' Jake answered before he could even stop himself.

Even the closing soirée had been hell, being back in that hotel ballroom. Everything had looked the same, from the same tablecloths to the same people in the same evening clothes.

But it hadn't been anywhere near the same. Because Flávia hadn't been there.

'Then why are we even here?' Brady demanded, yanking Jake back to the present.

That was a good question.

'It isn't as black and white as you think,' Jake began. 'There's your school, my job...'

He stopped, running out of excuses, and Brady

narrowed his eyes at him, for all the world looking at least twice his seven years.

'I hate this school, so what does it matter if I go to school out there instead? And if you really wanted to, you could change jobs and work out in Brazil.'

'Me going to work out there isn't that simple.' Jake shook his head, holding on to the only part that he could of what his young nephew had said. 'It's complicated.'

'Mummy always said that's what adults say when they don't want to explain something. I'm not a little kid,' he spat out.

'I know you like to think you're mature and understand life and the world around you,' Jake cut in firmly, shutting the conversation down. 'But that's exactly what you are, Brady—*a kid*. Something you have to understand is that adults know more than you do. And that we know what's best.'

'This is so unfair!' Brady cried, but at least the conversation was over.

So why did he feel so bad about it?

It felt like they'd made such progress in their relationship whilst they'd been in Brazil, but returning home had cost them, had propelled it all backwards.

Far from the engaged, social boy that his nephew had been when Flávia was around, as soon as they'd got home to London, Brady had started locking himself in his room and working on projects alone. No amount of cajoling had brought him out—not even Oz's famous cooking—and all the nature programmes that Jake had sat watching, just so that he could keep connecting with his nephew, was going to waste.

And he needed Flávia. Though not to resolve the problem for Brady...so much as to resolve the problem with himself.

How many times had he replayed that last conversation, trying to read every nuance? Trying to understand the fear which had made him say what he'd said. Words which, in his head, had sounded so logical and well-considered, but which had haunted him as a mistake ever since.

But there was one other thing stuck in his head.

Flávia's expression when she'd been talking to the doctor, and then the way she'd looked at him.

There had been something there—something he'd missed—but no matter how many times he replayed it, Jake couldn't get a handle on it.

His mind was still stuck on it when he pulled the car into the drive and shut off the engine to talk to Brady, but the boy was already snatching at the lever, practically hurling himself out of the vehicle and racing to the front door when he jabbed his finger at the hi-tech security lock.

Jake was fractions of a second away from letting Brady just run away when an image of Flávia popped into his head. A memory of her crouched down in front of the boy, talking to him on the same level, never dismissing his opinions or feelings.

With a sigh, he followed Brady up the stairs. He couldn't give up. He wouldn't.

Jake raked his hand through his hair and stared at the solid piece of wood as though willing it to open in front of his very eyes.

Maybe for Flávia it would have done so. But it didn't open for him.

He lifted his hand, second-guessed himself, and then—at last—he knocked on Brady's door, trying to affect an upbeat tone.

'You okay in there, mate?'

The door opened unexpectedly, nearly making Jake stumble back in surprise. A piece of paper was thrust out.

'I need you to give this to Flávia.'

'Flávia?' Even her name made something leap inside of him. 'You want me to send this to her?'

'No.' Brady clucked his tongue irritably. 'I want you to *give* this to her when you *see* her. It'll mean more.'

Jake raked his hand through his hair.

'I told you, I won't be seeing her again, Brady.'

'Why not?' Brady looked mutinous.

'Because I won't be returning to Brazil.'

There was no reason for his heart to thud so

heavily, so leaden, in his chest at the finality of the statement. No reason at all.

'Why can't you be a surgeon out there? They have hospitals, too.'

Jake was sure he could actually hear Flávia's voice in his head, light and happy, telling him to keep cool. He gritted his teeth and tried to sound understanding.

'You know the answer.'

'If you really wanted to, you could change your job.' Brady looked so sad, so lost, that Jake's chest pulled—taut and painful. 'I'd rather be out there than back here.'

The worst of it was that Jake felt the same way. For a long moment, the two of them stood in their respective positions, eyeing each other up.

If he was going to win back the connections they'd started to make in Brazil, then it occurred to him that he was going to have to be a little more truthful with Brady.

'Flávia is incredible. She made an impact on both of us—her whole family did—and I understand why you want to go back there. But I'm trying to protect you. You might not understand now but, trust me, one day you will.'

He sounded like those clichéd films, but what else was he supposed to say to a seven-year-old kid? He could hardly go into detail, could he?

Brady eyed him critically, his small brow furrowing into tight lines.

'Because she got bitten by a snake?'

Jake hesitated. He hadn't thought Brady had known, but he supposed it was too much to think that he hadn't been talking about it with Julianna and Marcie. Typical of Brady to keep it inside all this time, though.

'That's part of it,' he acknowledged at last.

'Were you frightened she might die? Like Mummy?'

God, the kid is too astute for his own good sometimes.

It took him a while to answer.

'Yes, mate. I was.'

'Me, too,' Brady whispered.

Without warning, the boy took a step forward and threw his arms around Jake's waist. Startled, it took Jake a moment to react, but when he did, it felt like the last obstacles between them were starting to crumble away.

And Flávia was somehow at the centre of it all again.

'That's why I don't think it's a good idea to go back out there,' Jake said after he'd carried the boy downstairs and settled him on the couch.

Maybe it was time to do what Flávia had kept suggesting, and talk.

'Why?' Brady pressed, and Jake drew in a steadying breath.

'Well, what if we did? What if we had Flávia in our lives and she got bitten again? And what if she didn't get better this time?'

'You mean, what if she died?' Brady looked at him solemnly.

The thought was sickening, but Jake forced himself to answer.

'Yeah, mate. What if she did?'

His nephew continued to gaze at him, solemn and unblinking.

'What if she didn't?' he asked at last. 'But, what if we stayed here and then you got sick, like Mummy, and you died. Who would look after me then? I don't want to live with Grandma and Granddad. I know I'm not supposed to say it, but I don't like them.'

'Is that what you think about?' Jake demanded.

It made sense, he supposed, given all that the kid had been through. But he hated that he hadn't realised Brady feared it. Hadn't thought about it.

No doubt Flávia had. That was yet another reason why she had been so good for them.

Still, doing it for Brady wasn't a good enough reason to go out to Brazil. If he was going to fight for Flávia, then he'd better be damned sure he was doing it for the right reasons.

And the simple truth was that he was.

Brady was right, of course. He could use Flávia's career as an excuse for anything if it suited him, and it had, because he'd been afraid of the way he felt about her. He'd spent so many years detaching himself from feeling anything that he'd refused to admit what had been staring him in the face.

She'd broken defences he hadn't even known he'd had, and she'd helped him connect with his nephew in a way he would never have managed left to his own devices. She'd mellowed him. More than that, she'd thawed him.

And it had taken Brady's boldness to stop him from being so scared of admitting it.

Carefully, thoughtfully, Jake turned the paper slowly around and looked at it. A frog?

'What is it, anyway?'

'She'll know what it means.'

'Right.' Jake pressed his lips together.

To his surprise, Brady relented slightly.

'It's a strawberry poison dart frog, and it's a super-parent. Just like Flávia.'

'It's perfect for her.' Jake grinned conspiratorially. 'So I guess we'd better book a couple of plane tickets and go and give it to her.'

CHAPTER FOURTEEN

Passport. Tickets. Money. Check.

Flávia lowered her small cabin bag onto the ground and wheeled it out into the corridor. She was locking the door to her apartment when she heard the *ping* of the lift doors opening out of sight. But there was no way she could have anticipated seeing Jake walk around the corner.

Everything stopped. Her legs. Her heart. Her brain.

She had no idea how long she stood there, immobile, just watching him stride up the corridor towards her.

'Going somewhere?'

His dry, sure voice floated in the air, and then everything kick-started inside her again, with a jolt.

'What are you doing back here?' She was running hot, then cold, then hot again, and she barely recognised her own voice.

'I'm back here for you,' he responded simply, and the certain, unequivocal nature of it seemed to steal her breath away.

'Why?' she demanded hoarsely as emotions

spiralled through her, too fast and too many to grasp.

But she recognised one of them. *Hope*. Why else would Jake be here, if not for her? Yet, at the same time, she could remember with painful clarity all the things they'd said to each other before he'd left Brazil last time.

And she knew the one thing he didn't. That she was carrying his baby.

'I'm guessing for the same reason you were heading to London.'

It was so simple, so direct, it made her heart stop for a second time in as many moments.

'How do you know?'

He half shrugged.

'I went to your sister's house as soon as I landed, thinking you'd either be in the rainforest or there. She told me.'

Her heart raced. Or stopped. She wasn't sure which.

'What else did she tell you?'

'That she was glad I'd come. That I should leave Brady with her whilst I found you, and that whatever else happened I should know that much.'

'I see,' Flávia managed, for want of anything better to say.

And then he moved closer, the air around them drawing that much thicker, that much tighter.

'I don't think you do see, Flávia,' he rasped. 'Not completely. And that's my fault for not saying it before. For not having the guts to say it before.'

'To say *what* before?'

He didn't answer, leaving her heart to thud. Long and slow and heavy.

'You told me that you couldn't put your desires ahead of Brady's needs,' she pressed on eventually. 'And I understand that. I get it.'

Jake took another step forward, his eyes holding hers so that she couldn't have dragged them away even if she'd wanted to.

'Only, what I feel for you is more than mere *desire*,' he murmured. 'It's much deeper than that.'

She wasn't sure when her soul left her body, but it was almost as though she was floating above the scene. Watching herself having this conversation, but too numb—too wound up with desperate anticipation—to actually feel part of it.

'Then…what?'

'I love you, Flávia Maura,' he told her simply, as if he hadn't just flipped her entire world upside down. Inside out. 'I can't imagine my life without you.'

Heat shot through Flávia's chest, plunging it into fire, like ramming it into a blast furnace. Then, just as quickly, doused it in an icy shower.

'Wait, Jake, before you say anything—'

'No, I waited before when I shouldn't have. I should have told you, because the simple truth is that I love you, but I'm not asking you to give up what you do. I know that makes you who you are. My fears were that something would happen to you, but I've come to see—actually, Brady has helped me to see—that those fears are for me to deal with. Not for you.'

'You don't understand—' she began, until Jake cut her off again.

'I can't subject you to a life where you spend every waking day in a lab, unable to escape into the rainforest, or spend time in that sanctuary which is so precious to you. I won't be the kind of man who does that—that isn't love. Not when I know who you are, and I understand what makes you tick. That is to say, I'm beginning to understand, and I truly can't wait to learn more about you. Every single day.'

'So…what are you saying, Jake?'

'I'm saying that I'm moving to Brazil. I've spoken to the board and we've started the ball rolling on the necessary procedures.'

It was more than she could ever have hoped for. Of course, guilt would have to hold her back. And it wasn't that protective armour she'd pulled around herself for years. It wasn't about her at all. It was about the baby that she hadn't even told him existed.

He might be saying all these things now, but how would he feel when he realised what she'd kept from him? Panic surged through her.

'You can't…' Every syllable quavered. She desperately fought against getting her hopes up, in case he hated her once he knew the truth. 'You said it yourself. Brady has to be your priority.'

'Brady loves you. He has made it unequivocally clear where his heart lies. And, like mine, it's very definitely out here. With you. You connected with him in days, in a way that I never could in almost ten months. He never came close to trusting me the way he trusts you. And Maria and her family, for that matter. You've made me realise that family is more important than anything. A good one, anyway.'

Flávia couldn't take it any more.

'Stop, Jake. Please, you have to stop.' Swinging around, she fumbled with the lock before pushing the door open wide. 'There's something you deserve—need—to know.'

Then, because there was no other way to say it than to be honest with him—finally—Flávia simply blurted it out.

'I'm pregnant.'

If she had slammed him in the gut, he wasn't sure it would have winded him any more than he already was.

He stared at her. Numb. Disbelieving. He waited for the betrayal to kick in, but although there was something there, it never quite kicked in.

'Pregnant?' It was him speaking, but he didn't recognise his voice.

'Yes,' she whispered.

'How? When?'

'You need me to run you through the mechanics of creating a baby?'

She was trying to brazen it out, that much was obvious. But the quake in her tone betrayed her. He couldn't answer, but his eyes never left hers until, abruptly, she slid her gaze away, her cheeks flushed.

'Possibly from that day we returned from the rainforest that first time. And it was the only time we didn't use protection.'

The time in the pool house, he remembered. Only too vividly. And now he was going to be a father.

Again, if he counted Brady, because for all intents and purposes, he was the closest thing the boy was going to have to a father.

'How long have you known?'

'Ever since the doctor told me in the hospital room that day. It was extremely early days, usually too early to tell, but I guess this little guy or girl was a fighter from the start.'

'I was in the room,' he realised with sudden clarity, and felt a tremor of impatience. But nothing like he might have expected.

That was the moment that had replayed in his head all this time. And then another thought slammed brutally into him.

'The bushmaster bite...?'

'The baby seems fine.' She practically fell over her words. 'I had tests and so far everything has checked out, but they're monitoring it.'

'I have a contact,' he growled, pulling out his mobile and beginning to punch in numbers. 'I met him this summer.'

'It's fine. I have someone already.'

He wasn't prepared for the way she placed her hand out to stop him. The contact seared straight through him.

'Why didn't you tell me? As soon as it happened?'

'I don't know.' She dropped her shoulders, her eyes meeting his imploringly. 'I was going to, but I didn't know how to. And then...'

'And then I told you that I couldn't put Brady through losing someone else he was close to,' he realised, and Flávia nodded awkwardly.

'But still...'

It was odd, but he couldn't quite decide how he felt. Both about the baby, and about the fact that Flávia had concealed the pregnancy from him.

'I didn't know if the baby was going to be all right at that point. Also, I didn't want you staying out of duty. Then resenting me.'

'I should never have put you in that position,' he rasped, because it was finally starting to sink in.

'You were looking out for Brady. I can understand that.' She shook her head, and he couldn't bring himself to elucidate.

Not yet. Not until he knew exactly what he wanted to say.

'I have to go into Paulista's. There's someone I need to speak to. Fancy a ride?'

She looked at him as though she was about to say something, then changed her mind.

'Sure.' She shrugged. 'They'll be surprised to see me here when I'm meant to be on a plane to London, but they won't complain.'

Jake took her keys, unlocked her door and deposited her cabin bag back inside, trying to make sense of these emotions sloshing around inside him. Was he angry or happy? He couldn't be sure. And until he was, he didn't want to confuse the issue.

He just knew he wanted to find a solution. Quickly.

Flávia left her lab late that evening, her mobile phone in her hand and the text from Jake still illuminating the screen.

She'd spent the day working since Jake had been in with the board all day and, to some degree, it had been a relief. At least it had distracted her from all the worries racing around her head.

Jake hadn't been furious as she might have expected when she'd told him about the baby, and she'd initially taken that to be a good sign.

Now, she wasn't so sure. What if it meant that he didn't care?

Trudging through the corridors, she pushed open the door to the car park and looked for his rental car, her heart nonetheless leaping as she saw him leaning on the bonnet. His impossibly masculine chest was shown off to perfection in a fitted shirt. Had he gone to a hotel room to clean up and change? Because that certainly wasn't what he'd been wearing this morning.

She edged nearer, her low heels tapping on the ground.

'Fruitful day?' he asked, his even tone giving nothing away.

'I guess,' she hedged. 'You?'

'Very.' And she thought she saw a quirk of his lips, but she couldn't be sure.

'Jake, listen, I should have said something this morning. Just so you know. But I knew I wanted this baby from the second I realised I was pregnant.'

'That's good to hear.' He dipped his head.

It wasn't the clearest of signals, but she'd take whatever she could.

'And I know I told you about the rainforest being my life, and the way my mother was, but I don't know if you understand how it relates. I don't know if *I* even understood it before.'

'But you do now?'

'I think I do,' she began. 'I told you that I was always…*different* as a kid, you've heard that before. The rainforest fascinated me from before I could even walk or talk. But when my mother walked out on us, I threw myself into it with everything I had. Maybe I thought fighting for a cause, taking on pet projects, gave me a place in life. I wanted to make a difference. I think I felt it made me relevant. Less disposable. Whatever, it became my life.'

'There's nothing wrong with that. What you do *matters*. You make a difference, Flávia.'

'Yes, and that was who I was. Without it, I feared I was no one. When I met Enrico, I thought my priorities would shift. I'd never give up my career, but I'd embrace being a wife. I'd want a family.'

'But you didn't.' He shrugged. 'That isn't who you are. It doesn't matter, we'll find a solution.'

'No, you don't understand.' She smiled. The realisation that Jake wanted to work through it with her buoyed her more than it had any right to. 'I was afraid that I was like *her*.'

'Your mother?'

She jerked her head in a semblance of a nod, but she couldn't bring herself to say it.

'I hated myself for it, but I couldn't make myself feel any of the things I thought I should. All the things Enrico wanted me to feel. And I thought it was my fault. For two years, I thought it was my fault. And then I met you.'

Jake moved closer to her. She could feel the heat, the energy, coming off him, pouring into her. The most glorious feeling she'd ever had.

'Even from that first night—our attempt at a one-night stand—I started to feel things for you that I'd never once felt for Enrico. But you were on the summer programme, you would be leaving, so I told myself that I was being ridiculous.'

'And do you still think that?' he demanded, his voice thick, a half-smile curving that all-too-tempting mouth of his.

She forced herself to stay focused.

'Who knows? I only know that I was ready to give up my life here, in order to follow you to the UK, before I even knew you would have me. Before I knew I was pregnant.'

'And now that you're pregnant?'

'Now I don't want to do anything to ever risk my baby, or myself. I love my career, but I want to be a mother, too. A good mother. A loving mother. I don't resent my baby. I can't want to meet it. Him. Her. I don't care.' A giddy laugh escaped her at the mere thought.

'Well, if it's confession time, then I guess I should make one to you,' he surprised her by saying. 'This morning, you told me that I was only looking out for Brady, but the fact is that I was looking out for myself, too. It suited me to hide behind Brady rather than acknowledge this multitude of...*feelings* I have for you.'

'You really do?' she breathed.

He loved that she sounded so breathless. So filled with anticipation.

'I really do,' he confirmed.

'That's good, because I'd almost started to think this morning was a hallucination. Too perfect to be true.'

'You're carrying my baby. Which only means that you belong with me. For ever.'

'For ever,' she echoed softly, almost a question.

And finally, Jake stepped forward and took her face in his hands, an infinitely tender gesture.

Then he lowered his head and kissed her. Slow, deep, intense. And she wrapped her arms around him, held him close and gave herself up to every exquisite second of it.

A second chance she had feared she would never get.

And then, when the kiss finally ended and he set her slightly back from him, Jake moved to the side, gesturing to the small copse of trees in the near distance. Rubber figs, flooded gums, blue gums. And suddenly, in amongst them, she spotted a shadowed area and her eyes narrowed instinctively.

A sleep system, with a basher and hammock, swayed lightly in the breeze. And little lights besides.

'What is this?' she breathed.

'Go and find out,' suggested Jake, so sure, so confident, that it sent a current of electricity pulsing through her veins.

Flávia had no idea how her shaking legs carried her over to the area. She only cared that she got there. And when she did, she realised the lights were tiny, twinkly, solar-powered stars.

'Not that it can ever compare to the canopy of stars in the jungle.'

'When the trees aren't so dense they cover it.' She laughed as best she could when she could barely breathe.

She was nervous, yet she didn't know why. Carefully, she slid to sit on the hammock. More for something to do than anything else.

'Pretty good,' she managed. 'Though there's only room for one.'

'I'm fine here,' he told her, his voice sounding even more strange.

And then he dropped on one knee and she realised he'd pulled a box out in front of her, and her heart stopped. Or raced. She couldn't quite tell.

She'd spent the day thinking he was discussing a patient case, wondering if he'd even remembered she was here. Instead, it seemed he'd been racing around getting changed, buying a ring and setting up this scenario.

As though nothing else had been on his mind but her. It was touching.

'Flávia Maura, you are the most complex, complicated woman I've ever known. And yet, you're also the most genuine and straightforward. You've been stealing your way inside a heart which I didn't even know I had, ever since the first moment. You make me feel things I've never before felt in my life, and now I know what it's like, I can't ever imagine going back.'

'Me, either,' she whispered.

Her head was spinning and twisting so fast it might as well have been on a coaster ride. Everything he was saying was almost too much. Too dreamlike. Too perfect.

'I don't see my life without you in it.' And she loved that it sounded more like a vow. 'And I know for a fact that Brady feels the same. You saved me, Flávia. You saved both of us and I love you. Marry me.'

'I love you, too,' she choked out. 'Yes. Yes, I'll marry you.'

Then, as Jake slid the most stunningly simple ring onto her finger, she realised she had never, ever felt so complete—*so right*—before. This time, when he drew her into his arms and kissed her, she knew it would never end.

This wasn't an end. This was just a beginning. And she couldn't wait to start the rest of her life with the man who had saved her just as much as he told her she had saved him.

They were married a month later in a quiet, closed ceremony in the botanical gardens where they had first got together. Eduardo gave her away, whilst Brady shared the responsibility of best man with an astonished Oz.

Julianna and Marcie were possibly the most excited bridesmaids in the history of weddings, whilst their mother cried enough tears to replenish the Amazon River. They had about thirty guests, including Cesar, Raoul and Fabio, and everyone cried a little, drank some wine and danced a lot.

The Maura-Cooper family welcomed their fourth member six months after that, on a glorious spring morning when the sun couldn't have shone any brighter.

Antonia Maura-Cooper came into the world with a battle cry fit for trailblazer, and Jake took her in his arms and gazed at her with such unadulterated love that Flávia's heart swelled so much she feared it might shatter.

And then he shifted his gaze to her and she felt as though she was the most powerful woman in the world.

* * * * *

*Look out for the previous story in the
A Summer in São Paulo trilogy*

Awakened by Her Brooding Brazilian
by Ann McIntosh

*And there is another fabulous story to come!
Available June 2020*

*If you enjoyed this story, check out these other
great reads from Charlotte Hawkes*

**Surprise Baby for the Billionaire
Unwrapping the Neurosurgeon's Heart
The Army Doc's Baby Secret
A Surgeon for the Single Mom**

All available now!